W9-BIV-101

She Was His Best Friend.

But in the back of Jason's mind, lying in wait all these years, was curiosity. What would it be like between them?

"I've been thinking about it all afternoon and decided I'd be a pretty lousy friend if I wasn't there when you needed me."

A broad smile transformed her expression. "You don't know how much this means to me. I'll call the clinic tomorrow and make an appointment for you."

Jason shook his head. "No fertility clinic. No doctor." He hooked his fingers around the sash that held her robe closed and tugged her a half step closer. Heat pooled below his belt at the way her lips parted in surprise. "Just you and me."

Something like excitement flickered in her eyes, only to be dampened by her frown. "Are you suggesting what I think you're suggesting?"

"Let's make a baby the old-fashioned way."

Dear Reader,

When I set out to write a friends-to-lovers book I had no idea of the challenges involved in helping best friends since first grade find their forever love.

Jason and Ming have been there for each other through every challenge and success. They bring out the best in each other. Or they did until romance entered the picture.

Deciding to take a chance on love is not always easy, and it's even worse for Ming and Jason because they risk losing their best friend if the relationship goes wrong. I hope you enjoy their journey from friends to forever.

All the best!

Cat Schield

CAT SCHIELD

A TRICKY PROPOSITION

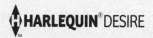

HARLEQUIN® DESIRE

If you purchased this book without a cover you should be aware
that this book is stolen property. It was reported as "unsold and
destroyed" to the publisher, and neither the author nor the
publisher has received any payment for this "stripped book."

Recycling programs
for this product may
not exist in your area.

ISBN-13: 978-0-373-73227-2

A TRICKY PROPOSITION

Copyright © 2013 by Catherine Schield

All rights reserved. Except for use in any review, the reproduction
or utilization of this work in whole or in part in any form by any
electronic, mechanical or other means, now known or hereafter
invented, including xerography, photocopying and recording, or in
any information storage or retrieval system, is forbidden without
the written permission of the publisher, Harlequin Enterprises Limited,
225 Duncan Mill Road, Don Mills, Ontario M3B 3K9, Canada.

This is a work of fiction. Names, characters, places and incidents are
either the product of the author's imagination or are used fictitiously, and
any resemblance to actual persons, living or dead, business establishments,
events or locales is entirely coincidental.

This edition published by arrangement with Harlequin Books S.A.

For questions and comments about the quality of this book, please contact us
at CustomerService@Harlequin.com.

® and TM are trademarks of Harlequin Enterprises Limited or its corporate
affiliates. Trademarks indicated with ® are registered in the United States Patent
and Trademark Office, the Canadian Trade Marks Office and in other countries.

Printed in U.S.A.

www.Harlequin.com

Books by Cat Schield

Harlequin Desire

Meddling with a Millionaire #2094
A Win-Win Proposition #2116
Unfinished Business #2153
The Rogue's Fortune #2192
A Tricky Proposition #2214

Other titles by this author available in ebook format.

CAT SCHIELD

has been reading and writing romance since high school. Although she graduated from college with a B.A. in business, her idea of a perfect career was writing books for Harlequin. And now, after winning the Romance Writers of America 2010 Golden Heart Award for series contemporary romance, that dream has come true. Cat lives in Minnesota with her daughter, Emily, and their Burmese cat. When she's not writing sexy, romantic stories for Harlequin Desire, she can be found sailing with friends on the St. Croix River or in more exotic locales like the Caribbean and Europe. She loves to hear from readers. Find her at www.catschield.com. Follow her on Twitter @catschield.

To my best friend, Annie Slawik.
I can't thank you enough for all the laughter and support.
Without you I wouldn't be who I am.

One

Ming Campbell's anxiety was not soothed by the restful trickle of water from the nearby fountain or by the calming greenery hanging from baskets around the restaurant's outdoor seating area. With each sip of her iced pomegranate tea she grew more convinced she was on the verge of making the biggest mistake of her life.

Beneath the table, her four-pound Yorkshire terrier lifted her chin off Ming's toes and began her welcome wiggle. Muffin might not be much of a guard dog, but she made one hell of an early warning system.

Stomach tightening, Ming glanced up. A tall man in loose-fitting chinos, polo shirt and casual shoes approached. Sexy stubble softened his chiseled cheeks and sharp jaw.

"Sorry I'm late."

Jason Sterling's fingertips skimmed her shoulder, sending a rush of goose bumps speeding down her arm. Ming cursed her body's impulsive reaction as he sprawled in the chair across from hers.

Ever since breaking off her engagement to his brother, Evan, six months ago, she'd grown acutely conscious of any and all contact with him. The friendly pat he gave her arm. His shoulder bumping hers as he sat beside her on the couch. The affable hugs he doled so casually that scrambled her nerve endings. It wasn't as if she could tell him to stop. He'd want to know what was eating at her, and there was no way she was going to tell him. So, she silently endured and hoped the feelings would go away or at least simmer down.

Muffin set her front paws on his knee, her brown eyes fixed on his face, and made a noise that was part bark, part sneeze. Jason slid his hand beneath the terrier's belly and lifted her so she could give his chin a quick lick. That done, the dog settled on his lap and heaved a contented sigh.

Jason signaled the waitress and they ordered lunch. "How come you didn't start without me?"

Because she was too keyed up to be hungry. "You said you were only going to be fifteen minutes late."

Jason was the consummate bachelor. Self-involved, pre-occupied with amateur car racing and always looking for the next bit of adventure, whether it was a hot girl or a fast track. They'd been best friends since first grade and she loved him, but that didn't mean he didn't occasionally drive her crazy.

"Sorry about that. We hit some traffic just as we got back into town."

"I thought you were coming home yesterday."

"That was the plan, but then the guys and I went out for a couple beers after the race and our celebration went a little long. None of us were in any shape to drive five hours back to Houston." With a crooked smile he extended his long legs in front of him and set his canvas-clad foot on the leg of her chair.

"How is Max taking how far you are ahead of him in points?" The two friends had raced domestic muscle cars in events sanctioned by the National Auto Sports Association since they were sixteen. Each year they competed to see who could amass the most points.

"Ever since he got engaged, I don't think he cares."

She hadn't seen Jason this disgruntled since his dad fell for a woman twenty years his junior. "You poor baby. Your best buddy has grown up and gotten on with his life, leaving you behind." Ming set her elbow on the table and dropped her chin into her palm. She'd been listening to Jason complain about the changes in his best friend ever since Max Case had proposed to the love of his life.

Jason leaned forward, an intense look in his eyes. "Maybe I need to find out what all the fuss is about."

"I thought you were never going to get married." Sudden anxiety crushed the air from her lungs. If he fell madly in love with someone, the dynamic of their friendship would change. She'd no longer be his best "girl" friend.

"No worries about that." His lopsided grin eased some of her panic.

Ming turned her attention to the Greek salad the waitress set in front of her. In high school she'd developed a crush on Jason. It had been hopeless. Unrequited. Except for one brief interlude after prom—and he'd taken pains to assure her that had been a mistake—he'd never given her any indication that he thought of her as anything but a friend.

When he headed off to college, time and distance hadn't blunted her feelings for him, but it had provided her with perspective. Even if by some miracle Jason did fall madly in love with her, he wasn't going to act on it. Over and over, he'd told her how important her friendship was to him and how he didn't want to do anything to mess that up.

"So, what's up?" Jason said, eyeing her over the top of his hamburger. "You said you had something serious to discuss with me."

And in the thirty minutes she'd sat waiting for him, she'd

talked herself into a state of near panic. Usually she told him everything going on in her life. Well, almost everything.

When she'd starting dating Evan there were a few topics they didn't discuss. Her feelings for his brother being the biggest. Holding her own council about such an enormous part of her life left her feeling as if a chunk of her was missing, but she'd learned to adjust and now found it harder than she expected to open up to him.

"I'm going to have a baby." She held her breath and waited for his reaction.

A French fry paused midway between his plate and his mouth. "You're pregnant?"

She shook her head, some of her nervousness easing now that the conversation had begun. "Not yet."

"When?"

"Hopefully soon."

"How? You're not dating anyone."

"I'm using a clinic."

"Who's going to be the father?"

She dodged his gaze and stabbed her fork into a kalamata olive. "I've narrowed the choices down to three. A lawyer who specializes in corporate law, an athlete who competes in the Ironman Hawaii challenge every year and a wildlife photographer. Brains. Body. Soul. I haven't decided which way to go yet."

"You've obviously been thinking about this for a while. Why am I only hearing about it now?" He pushed his plate away, abandoning his half-eaten burger.

In the past she'd been able to talk to Jason about anything. Getting involved with his brother had changed that. Not that it should have. She and Jason were friends with no hope of it ever being anything more.

"You know why Evan and I broke up." She'd been troubled that Evan hadn't shared her passion for family, but she thought he'd come around. "Kids are important to me. I wouldn't do what I do if they weren't."

She'd chosen to become an orthodontist because she loved kids. Their sunny view of the world made her smile, so she gave them perfect teeth to smile back.

"Have you told your parents?"

"Not yet." She shifted on her chair.

"Because you know your mother won't react well to you getting pregnant without being married."

"She won't like it, but she knows how much I want a family of my own, and she's come to accept that I'm not going to get married."

"You don't know that. Give yourself a chance to get over your breakup with Evan. There's someone out there for you."

Not likely when the only man she could see herself with was determined never to marry. Frustration bubbled up. "How long do I wait? Another six months? A year? In two months I turn thirty-two. I don't want to waste any more time weighing the pros and cons or worrying about my mom's reaction when in my heart I know what I want." She thrust out her chin. "I'm going to do this, Jason."

"I can see that."

Mesmerizing eyes studied her. Galaxy blue, the exact shade of her '66 Shelby Cobra convertible. He'd helped her convince her parents to buy the car for her seventeenth birthday and then they'd spent the summer restoring it. She had fond memories of working with him on the convertible, and every time she drove it, she couldn't help but feel connected to Jason. That's why she'd parked the car in her garage the day she started dating his brother and hadn't taken it out since.

"I'd really like you to be on board with my decision."

"You're my best friend," he reminded her, eyes somber. "How can I be anything but supportive?"

Even though she suspected he was still processing her news and had yet to decide whether she was making a mistake, he'd chosen to back her. Ming relaxed. Until that second she hadn't realized how anxious she was about Jason's reaction.

"Are you done eating?" she asked a few minutes later, catching the waitress's eye. Jason hadn't finished his lunch and showed no signs of doing so. "I should probably get back to the clinic. I have a patient to see in fifteen minutes."

He snagged the bill from the waitress before she set it on the table and pulled out his wallet.

"I asked you to lunch." Ming held her hand out imperiously. "You are not buying."

"It's the least I can do after being so late. Besides, the way you eat, you're always a cheap date."

"Thanks."

While Jason slipped cash beneath the saltshaker, she stood and called Muffin to her. The Yorkie refused to budge from Jason's lap. Vexed, Ming glared at the terrier. She was not about to scoop the dog off Jason's thighs. Her pulse hitched at the thought of venturing anywhere near his muscled legs.

Air puffing out in a sigh, she headed for the wood gate that led directly to the parking lot. Jason was at her side, dog tucked beneath his arm, before she reached the pavement.

"Where's your car?" he asked.

"I walked. It's only two blocks."

Given that humidity wasn't a factor on this late-September afternoon, she should have enjoyed her stroll to the restaurant. But what she wanted to discuss with Jason had tied her up in knots.

"Come on. I'll drive you back." He took her hand, setting off a shower of sparks that heightened her senses.

The spicy scent of his cologne infiltrated her lungs and caused the most disturbing urges. His warm, lean body bumped against her hip. It was moments like these when she was tempted to call her receptionist and cancel her afternoon appointments so she could take Jason home and put an end to all the untidy lust rampaging through her body.

Of course, she'd never do that. She'd figure out some other way to tame the she-wolf that had taken up residence beneath her skin. All their lives she'd been the conservative one. The one who studied hard, planned for the future, organized her life down to the minute. Jason was the one who acted on impulse. Who partied his way through college and still managed to graduate with honors. And who liked his personal life unfettered by anyone's expectations.

They neared his car, a 1969 Camaro, and Jason stepped forward to open the passenger door for her. Being nothing more than friends didn't stop him from treating her with the same chivalry he afforded the women he dated. Before she could sit down he had to pluck an eighteen-inch trophy off her seat. Despite the cavalier way he tossed the award into the backseat, Ming knew the win was a source of pride to him and that the trophy would end up beside many others in his "racing" room.

"So what else is on your mind?" Jason asked, settling behind the wheel and starting the powerful engine. Sometimes he knew what she was thinking before she did.

"It's too much to get into now." She cradled Muffin in her arms and brushed her cheek against the terrier's silky coat. The dog gave her hand a happy lick.

"Give me the CliffsNotes version."

Jason accelerated out of the parking lot, the roar of the 427 V-8 causing a happy spike in Ming's heart rate. Riding shotgun in whatever Jason drove had been a thrill since the year he'd turned sixteen and gotten his first muscle car. Where other boys in school had driven relatively new cars, Jason and Max preferred anything fast from the fifties, sixties and seventies.

"It doesn't matter because I changed my mind."

"Changed your mind about what?"

"About what I was going to ask you." She wished he'd just drop it, but she knew better. Now that his curiosity had been aroused, he would bug her until he got answers. "It doesn't matter."

"Sure it does. You've been acting odd for weeks now. What's up?"

Ming sighed in defeat. "You asked me who was going to be the father." She paused to weigh the consequences of telling him. She'd developed a logical explanation that had nothing to do with her longing to have a deeper connection with him. He never had to know how she really felt. Her heart a battering ram against her ribs, she said, "I wanted it to be you."

Silence dominated until Jason stopped the car in front of the medical building's entrance. Ming's announcement smacked into him like the heel of her hand applied to his temple. That she wanted to have a baby didn't surprise him. It's what had broken up her and Evan. But that she wanted Jason to be the father caught him completely off guard.

Had her platonic feelings shifted toward romance? Desire? Unlikely.

She'd been his best friend since first grade. The one person he'd let see his fear when his father had tried to commit suicide. The only girl who'd listened when he went on and on about his goals and who'd talked sense into him when doubts took hold.

In high school, girlfriends came and went, but Ming was always there. Smart and funny, her almond-shaped eyes glowing with laughter. She provided emotional support without complicating their relationship with exasperating expectations. If he canceled plans with her she never pouted or ranted. She never protested when he got caught up working on car engines or shooting hoops with his buddies and forgot to call her. And more often than not, her sagacity kept Jason grounded.

She would have made the perfect girlfriend if he'd been willing to ruin their twenty-five-year friendship for a few months of romance. Because eventually his eye would wander and she'd be left as another casualty of his carefully guarded heart.

He studied her beautiful oval face. "Why me?"

Below inscrutable black eyes, her full lips kicked up at the corners. "You're the perfect choice."

The uneasy buzz resumed in the back of his mind. Was she looking to change their relationship in some way? Link herself to him with a child? He never intended to marry. Ming knew that. Accepted it. Hadn't she?

"How so?"

"Because you're my best friend. I know everything about you. Something about having a stranger's child makes me uncomfortable." She sighed. "Besides, I'm perfectly comfortable being a single parent. You are a dedicated bachelor. You won't have a crisis of conscience and demand your parental rights. It's perfect."

"Perfect," he echoed, reasoning no matter what she claimed, a child they created together would connect them in a way that went way beyond friendship.

"You're right. I don't want marriage or kids. But fathering your child…" Something rumbled in his subconscious, warning him to stop asking questions. She'd decided against asking him to help her get pregnant. He should leave it at that.

"Don't say it that way. You're making it too complicated. We've been friends forever. I don't want anything to change our relationship."

Too late for that. "Things between us changed the minute you started dating Evan."

Jason hadn't welcomed the news. In fact, he'd been quite displeased, which was something he'd had no right to feel. If she was nothing more than his friend, he should have been happy that she and Evan had found each other.

"I know. In the beginning it was awkward, but I never would have gone out with him if you hadn't given me your blessing."

What other choice did he have? It wasn't as if he intended to claim her as anything other than a friend. But such rational thinking hadn't stood him in good stead the first time he'd seen his brother kiss her.

"You didn't need my blessing. If you wanted to date Evan, that was your business." And he'd backed off. Unfortunately, distance had lent him perspective. He'd begun to see her not only as his longtime friend, but also as a desirable woman. "But let's get back to why you changed your mind about wanting me."

"I didn't want *you*," she corrected, one side of her mouth twitching. "Just a few of your strongest swimmers."

She wanted to make light of it, but Jason wasn't ready to oblige her. "Okay, how come you changed your mind about wanting my swimmers?"

She stared straight ahead and played with the Yorkie's ears, sending the dog into a state of bliss. "Because we'd have to keep it a secret. If anyone found out what we'd done, it would cause all sorts of hard feelings."

Not anyone. Evan. She'd been hurt by his brother, yet she'd taken Evan's feelings into consideration when making such an important decision. She'd deserved better than his brother.

"What if we didn't keep it a secret? My dad would be thrilled that one of his sons made him a grandfather," Jason prompted.

"But he'd also expect you to be a father." Her eyes soft with understanding, she said, "I wouldn't ask that of you."

He resented her assumption that he wouldn't want to be involved. Granted, until ten minutes earlier he'd never considered being a parent, but suddenly Jason didn't like the idea that his child would never know him as his father. "I don't suppose I can talk you out of this."

"My mind is set. I'm going to have babies."

"Babies?" He ejected the word and followed it up with a muttered curse. "I thought it was a baby. Now you're fielding a baseball team?"

A goofy snort of laughter escaped her. Unattractive on ninety-nine percent of women, the sound was adorable erupting from her long, thin nose. It probably helped that her jet-black eyes glittered with mischief, inviting him to join in her amusement.

"What's so funny?" he demanded.

She shook her head, the action causing the ebony curtains of hair framing her exotic Asian features to sway like a group of Latin dancers doing a rumba. "You should see the look on your face."

He suppressed a growl. There was not one damn thing about this that was funny. "I thought this was a one-time deal."

"It is, but you never know what you're going to get when you go in vitro. I might have triplets."

Jason's thoughts whirled. "Triplets?" Damn. He hadn't adjusted to the idea of one child. Suddenly there were three?

"It's possible." Her gaze turned inward. A tranquil half smile curved her lips.

For a couple, triplets would be hard. How was she going to handle three babies as a single mom?

Images paraded through his head. Ming's mysterious smile as she placed his hand on her round belly. Her eyes sparkling as she settled the baby in his arms for the first time. The way the pictures appealed to him triggered alarm bells. After his father's suicide attempt, he'd closed himself off to being a husband and a father. Not once in the years since had he questioned his decision.

Ming glanced at the silver watch on her delicate wrist. "I've got seven minutes to get upstairs or I'll be late for my next appointment."

"We need to talk about this more."

"It'll have to be later." She gathered Muffin and exited the car.

"When later?"

But she'd shut the door and was heading away, sleek and sexy in form-fitting black pants and a sleeveless knit top that showed off her toned arms.

Appreciation slammed into his gut.

Uninvited.

Unnerving.

Cursing beneath his breath, Jason shut off the engine, got out of the car and headed for the front door, but he wasn't fast enough to catch her before she crossed the building's threshold.

Four-inch heels clicking on the tile lobby floor, she headed toward the elevator. With his longer legs, Jason had little trouble keeping pace. He reached the elevator ahead of her and put his hand over the up button to keep her from hitting it.

"The Camaro will get towed if you leave it there."

He barely registered her words. "Let's have dinner."

A ding sounded and the doors before them opened. She barely waited for the elevator to empty before stepping forward.

"I already have plans."

"With whom?"

She shook her head. "Since when are you so curious about my social life?"

Since her engagement had broken off.

On the third floor, they passed a door marked Dr. Terrance Kincaid, DDS, and Dr. Ming Campbell, DDS. Another ten feet and they came to an unmarked door that she unlocked and breezed through.

One of the dental assistants hovered outside Ming's office. "Oh, good, you're here. I'll get your next patient."

Ming set down Muffin, and the Yorkie bounded through the hallway toward the waiting room. She headed into her office and returned wearing a white lab coat. When she started past him, Jason caught her arm.

"You can't do this alone." Whether he meant get pregnant or raise a child, he wasn't sure.

Her gentle smile was meant to relieve him of all obligations. "I'll be fine."

"I don't doubt that." But he couldn't shake the sense that she needed him.

A thirteen-year-old boy appeared in the hallway and waved to her.

"Hello, Billy," she called. "How did your baseball tournament go last month?"

"Great. Our team won every game."

"I'd expect nothing else with a fabulous pitcher like you on the mound. I'll see you in a couple minutes."

As often as Jason had seen her at work, he never stopped being amazed that she could summon a detail for any of her two hundred clients that made the child feel less like a patient and more like a friend.

"I'll call you tomorrow." Without waiting for him to respond, she followed Billy to the treatment area.

Reluctant to leave, Jason stared after her until she disappeared. Impatience and concern urged him to hound her until he was satisfied he knew all her plans, but he knew how he'd feel if she'd cornered him at work.

Instead, he returned to the parking lot. The Camaro remained at the curb where he'd left it. Donning his shades, he slid behind the wheel and started the powerful engine.

Two

When Ming returned to her office after her last appointment, she found her sister sitting cross-legged on the floor, a laptop balanced on her thighs.

"There are three chairs in the room. You should use one."

"I like sitting on the ground." With her short, spiky hair and fondness for natural fibers and loose-fitting clothes, Lily looked more than an environmental activist than a top software engineer. "It lets me feel connected to the earth."

"We're three stories up in a concrete building."

Lily gave her a "whatever" shoulder shrug and closed the laptop. "I stopped by to tell you I'm heading out really early tomorrow morning."

"Where to this time?"

For the past five years, her sister had been leading a team of consultants involved with transitioning their company's various divisions to a single software system. Since the branches were all over the country, she traveled forty weeks out of the year. The rest of the time, she stayed rent-free in Ming's spare bedroom.

"Portland."

"How long?"

"They offered me a permanent position."

Her sister's announcement came as an unwelcome surprise. "Did you say yes?"

"Not yet. I want to see if I like Portland first. But I gotta tell you, I'm sick of all the traveling. It would be nice to buy a place and get some appliances. I want a juicer."

Lily had this whole "a healthy body equals a healthy mind" mentality. She made all sorts of disgusting green concoctions that smelled awful and tasted like a decomposing marsh. Ming's eyes watered just thinking about them. She preferred to jump-start her day with massive doses of caffeine.

"You won't get bored being stuck in one city?"

"I'm ready to settle down."

"And you can't settle down in Houston?"

"I want to meet a guy I can get serious about."

"And you have to go all the way to Portland to find one?" Ming wondered what was really going on with her sister.

Lily slipped her laptop into its protective sleeve. "I need a change."

"You're not going to stick around and be an auntie?" She'd hoped once Lily held the baby and saw how happy Ming was as a mom, her sister could finally get why Ming was willing to risk their mother's wrath about her decision.

"I think it's better if I don't."

As close as the sisters were, they'd done nothing but argue since Ming had divulged her intention of becoming a single mom. Her sister's negative reaction had come as a complete surprise. And on the heels of her broken engagement, Ming was feeling alone and blue.

"I wish I could make you understand how much this means to me."

"Look, I get it. You've always wanted children. I just think that a kid needs both a mother and a father."

Ming's confidence waned beneath her sister's criticism. Despite her free-spirited style and reluctance to be tied down, Lily was a lot more traditional than Ming when it came to family. Last night, when Ming had told her sister she was going to talk to Jason today, Lily had accused Ming of being selfish.

But was she? Raising a child without a father didn't necessarily mean that the child would have problems. Children needed love and boundaries. She could provide both.

It wasn't fair for Lily to push her opinions on Ming. She hadn't made her decision overnight. She'd spent months and months talking to single moms, weighing the pros and cons, and using her head, not her emotions, to make up her mind about raising a child on her own. Of course, when it came right down to it, her longing to be a mother was a strong, biological urge that was hard to ignore.

Ming slipped out of her lab coat and hung it on the back of her office door. "Have you told Mom about the job offer?"

"No." Lily countered. "Have you told her what you're going to do?"

"I was planning to on Friday. We're having dinner, just the two of us." Ming arched an eyebrow. "Unless you'd like to head over there now so we can both share our news. Maybe with two of us to yell at, we'll each get half a tongue lashing."

"As much as I would love to be there to see the look on Mom's face when she finds out you're going to have a baby without a husband, I'm not ready to talk about my plans. Not until I'm completely sure."

It sounded as if Lily wasn't one hundred percent sold on moving away. Ming kept relief off her face and clung to the hope that her sister would find that Portland wasn't to her liking.

"Will I see you at home later?"

Lily shook her head. "Got plans."

"A date?"

"Not exactly."

"Same guy?" For the past few months, whenever she was in town, her sister had been spending a lot of time with a mystery man. "Have you told him your plans to move?"

"It's not like that."

"It's not like what?"

"We're not dating."

"Then it's just sex?"

Her sister made an impatient noise. "Geez, Ming. You of all people should know that men and women can be just friends."

"Most men and women can't. Besides, Jason and I are more like brother and sister than friends."

For about the hundredth time, Ming toyed with telling Lily about her mixed feelings for Jason. How she loved him as a friend but couldn't stop wondering if they could have made it as a couple. Of course, she'd blown any chance to find out when she'd agreed to have dinner with Evan three years ago.

But long before that she knew Jason wouldn't let anything get in the way of their friendship.

"Have you told him about your plans to have a baby yet?"

"I mentioned it to him this afternoon."

She was equally disappointed and relieved that she'd decided against asking Jason to help her get pregnant. Raising his child would muddle her already complicated emotions where he was concerned. It would be easier to get over her romantic yearnings if she had no expectations.

"How did he take it?"

"Once he gets used to the idea, I think he'll be happy for me." Her throat locked up. She'd really been counting on his support.

"Maybe this is the universe's way of telling you that you're on the wrong path."

"I don't need the universe to tell me anything. I have you." Although Ming kept her voice light, her heart was heavy. She was torn between living her dream and disrupting her relationships with those she loved. What if this became a wedge between her and Lily? Or her and Jason? Ming hated the idea of being pulled in opposite directions by her longing to be a mom and her fear of losing the closeness she shared with either of them.

To comfort herself, she stared at her photo wall, the proof of what she'd achieved these past seven years. Hundreds of smiles lightened her mood and gave her courage.

"I guess you and I will just have to accept that neither one of us is making a decision the other is happy with," Ming said.

Jason paced from one end of his large office to the other. Beyond his closed door, the offices of Sterling Bridge Company emptied. It was a little past six, but Jason had given up working hours ago. As the chief financial officer of the family's bridge construction business, he was supposed to be looking over some last-minute changes in the numbers for a multimillion-dollar project they were bidding on next week, but he couldn't focus. Not surprising after Ming's big announcement today.

She'd be a great mom. Patient. Loving. Stern when she had to be. If he'd voiced doubts it wasn't because of her ability to parent, but how hard it would be for her to do it on her own. Naturally Ming wouldn't view any difficulty as too much trouble. She'd embrace the challenges and surpass everyone's expectations.

But knowing this didn't stop his uneasiness. His sense that he should be there for her. Help her.

Help her what?

Get pregnant.

Raise his child?

His gut told him it was the right thing to do even if his brain warned him that he was embarking on a fool's journey. They were best friends. This was when best friends stepped up and helped each other out. If the situation was reversed and he wanted a child, she'd be the woman he'd choose to make that happen.

But if they did this, things could get complicated. If his brother found out that Jason had helped Ming become a mother, the hurt they caused might lead to permanent estrangement between him and Evan.

On the other hand, Ming deserved to get the family she wanted.

Another thirty minutes disappeared with Jason lost in thought. Since he couldn't be productive at the office, he decided to head home. A recently purchased '73 Dodge Charger sat in his garage awaiting some TLC. In addition to his passion for racing, he loved buying, fixing up and selling classic muscle cars. It's why he'd chosen his house in the western suburbs. The three-acre estate had afforded him the opportunity to build a six-car garage to house his rare collection.

On the way out, Jason passed his brother's office. Helping Ming get pregnant would also involve keeping another big secret from his brother. Jason resented that she still worried about Evan's feelings after the way he'd broken off their engagement. Would it be as awkward for Evan to be an uncle to his ex-fiancée's child as it had been for Jason to watch his best friend fall in love with his brother?

From the moment Ming and Evan had begun dating, tension had developed between Jason and his brother. An unspoken rift that was territorial in nature. Ming and Jason were best friends. They were bonded by difficult experiences. Inside jokes. Shared memories. In the beginning, it was Evan who was the third wheel whenever the three of them got together. But this wasn't like other times when Ming had dated. Thanks to her long friendship with Jason, she was practically family. Within months, it was obvious she and Evan were perfectly matched in temperament and outlook, and the closer Ming and Evan became, the more Jason became the outsider. Which was something he resented. Ming was his best friend and he didn't like sharing her.

Entering his brother's office, Jason found Evan occupying the couch in the seating area. Evan was three years older and carried more weight on his six-foot frame than Jason, but otherwise, the brothers had the same blue eyes, dark blond hair and features. Both resembled their mother, who'd died in a car accident with their nine-year-old sister when the boys were in high school.

The death of his wife and daughter had devastated their father. Tony Sterling had fallen into a deep depression that lasted six months and almost resulted in the loss of his business. And if Jason hadn't snuck into the garage one night to "borrow" the car for a joyride and found his father sitting behind the wheel with the garage filling with exhaust fumes, Tony might have lost his life.

This pivotal event had happened when Jason was only fifteen years old and had marked him. He swore he would never succumb to a love so strong that he would be driven to take his own life when the love was snatched away. It had been an easy promise to keep.

Jason scrutinized his brother as he crossed the room, his footfalls soundless on the plush carpet. Evan was so focused on the object in his hand he didn't notice Jason's arrival until he spoke.

"Want to catch dinner?"

Evan's gaze shot toward his brother, and in a furtive move, he pocketed the earrings he'd been brooding over. Jason recognized them as the pearl-and-diamond ones his brother had given to Ming as an engagement present. What was his brother doing with them?

"Can't. I've already got plans."

"A date?"

Evan got to his feet and paced toward his desk. With his back to Jason, he spoke. "I guess."

"You don't know?"

That was very unlike his brother. When it came to living a meticulously planned existence, the only one more exacting than Evan was Ming.

Evan's hand plunged into the pocket he'd dropped the earrings into. "It's complicated."

"Is she married?"

"No."

"Engaged?"

"No."

"Kids?"

"Let it go." Evan's exasperation only increased Jason's tension.

"Does it have something to do with Ming's earrings in your pocket?" When Evan didn't answer, Jason's gut clenched, his suspicions confirmed. "Haven't you done enough damage there? She's moving on with her life. She doesn't need you stirring things up again."

"I didn't plan what happened. It just did."

Impulsive behavior from his plan-everything-to-death brother? Jason didn't like the sound of that. It could only lead to Ming getting hurt again.

"What exactly happened?"

"Lily and I met for a drink a couple months ago."

"You and Lily?" He almost laughed at the odd pairing. While Evan and Ming had been perfectly compatible, Evan and Lily were total opposites. Then he sobered. "Just the once?"

"A few times." Evan rubbed his face, bringing Jason's attention to the dark shadows beneath his eyes. His brother looked exhausted. And low. "A lot."

"Have you thought about what you're doing?" When it came to picking sides, Jason would choose Ming every time. In some ways, she was more like family to him than Evan. Jason had certainly shared more of himself with her. "Don't you think

Ming will be upset if she finds out you and her sister are dating?"

Before Evan could answer, Jason's cell began to ring. With Ming's heart in danger and his brother in his crosshairs, Jason wouldn't have allowed himself to be distracted if anyone else on the planet was calling. But this was Ming's ringtone.

"We'll talk more about this later," he told his brother, and answered the call as he exited. "What's going on?"

"It's Lily." There was no mistaking the cry for help in Ming's voice.

Jason's annoyance with his brother flared anew. Had Ming found out what was going on? "What about her?"

"She's moving to Portland. What am I going to do without her?"

What a relief. Ming didn't yet know that her sister was dating Evan, and if Lily moved to Portland then her relationship with her sister's ex-fiancé would have to end.

"You still have me." He'd intended to make his tone light, but on the heels of his conversation with his brother moments before, his declaration came out like a pledge. "Do you want to catch a drink and talk about it? We could continue our earlier conversation."

"I can't. Terry and I are having dinner."

"Afterward?"

"It's been a long day. I'm heading home for a glass of wine and a long, hot bath."

"Do you want some company?"

Unbidden, his thoughts took him to an intoxicating, sensual place where Ming floated naked in warm, fragrant water. Candles burned, setting her delicate, pale shoulders aglow above the framing bubbles of her favorite bath gel. The office faded away as he imagined trailing his lips along her neck, discovering all the places on her silky skin that made her shiver.

"Jason?" Ming's voice roused him to the fact that he was standing in the elevator. He didn't remember getting there.

Damn it. He banished the images, but the sensations lingered.

"What?" he asked, disturbed at how compelling his fantasy had been.

"I asked if I could call you later."

"Sure." His voice had gone hoarse. "Have a good dinner."

"Thanks."

The phone went dead in his hand. Jason dropped the cell back into his pocket, still reeling from the direction his thoughts had gone. He had to stop thinking of her like that. Unfortunately, once awakened, the notion of making love to Ming proved difficult to coax back to sleep.

He headed to his favorite bar, which promised a beer and a dozen sports channels as a distraction from his problems. It failed to deliver.

Instead, he replayed his conversations with both Ming and Evan in his mind. She wanted to have a baby, wanted Jason's help to make that happen, but she'd decided against it before he'd had a chance to consider the idea. All because it wouldn't be fair to Evan if he ever found out.

Would she feel the same if she knew Evan was dating Lily and that he didn't care if Ming got hurt in the process? That wouldn't change her mind. Even if it killed her, Ming would want Evan and Lily to be happy.

But shouldn't she get to be selfish, too? She should be able to choose whatever man she wanted to help her get pregnant. Even the brother of her ex-fiancé. Only Jason knew she'd never go there without a lot of convincing.

And wasn't that what best friends were for?

Fifteen minutes after she'd hung up on Jason, Ming's heart was still thumping impossibly fast. She'd told herself that when he'd asked if she wanted company for a glass of wine and a hot bath, he hadn't meant anything sexual. She'd called him for a shoulder to cry on. That's all he was offering.

But the image of him sliding into her oversize tub while candlelight flickered off the glass tile wall and a thousand soap bubbles drifted on the water's surface…

"Ready for dinner?"

Jerked out of her musing, Ming spun her chair away from her computer and spied Terry Kincaid grinning at her from the doorway, his even, white teeth dazzling against his tan skin. As well as being her partner in the dental practice and her best girl friend's father, he was the reason she'd chosen to become an orthodontist in the first place.

"Absolutely."

She closed her internet browser and images of strollers disappeared from her screen. As crazy as it was to shop for baby stuff before she was even pregnant, Ming couldn't stop herself from buying things. Her last purchase had been one of those mobiles that hangs above the crib and plays music as it spins.

"You already know how proud I am of you," Terry began after they'd finished ordering dinner at his favorite seafood place. "When I brought you into the practice, it wasn't because you were at the top of your class or a hard worker, but because you're like family."

"You know that's how I feel about you, too." In fact, Terry was so much better than her own family because he offered her absolute support without any judgment.

"And as a member of my family, it was important to me that I come to you with any big life-changing decisions I was about to make."

Ming gulped. How had he found out what she was going to do? Wendy couldn't have told him. Her friend knew how to keep a secret.

"Sure," she said. "That's only fair."

"That's why I'm here to tell you that I'm going to retire and I want you to take over the practice."

This was the last thing she expected him to say. "But you're only fifty-seven. You can't quit now."

"It's the perfect time. Janice and I want to travel while we're still young enough to have adventures."

In addition to being a competitive sailor, Terry was an expert rock climber and pilot. Where Ming liked relaxing spa vacations in northern California, he and his wife went hang gliding in Australia and zip lining through the jungles of Costa Rica.

"And you want me to have the practice?" Her mind raced at the thought of all the things she would have to learn, and fast. Managing personnel and finances. Marketing. The practice thrived with Terry at the helm. Could she do half as well? "It's a lot."

"If you're worried about the money, work the numbers with Jason."

"It's not the money." It was an overwhelming responsibility to take on at the same time she was preparing for the challenge of being a single mom. "I'm not sure I'm ready."

Terry was unfazed by her doubts. "I've never met anyone who rises to the challenge the way you do. And I'm not going to retire next week. I'm looking at the middle of next year. Plenty of time for you to learn what you need to know."

The middle of next year? Ming did some rapid calculation. If everything went according to schedule, she'd be giving birth about the time when Terry would be leaving. Who'd take over while she was out on maternity leave? She'd hoped for twelve glorious weeks with her newborn.

Yet, now that the initial panic was fading, excitement stirred. Her own practice. She'd be crazy to let this opportunity pass her by.

"Ming, are you all right?" Concern had replaced delight. "I thought you'd jump at the chance to run the practice."

"I'm really thrilled by the opportunity."

"But?"

She was going to have a baby. Taking over the practice would require a huge commitment of time and energy. But Terry believed in her and she hated to disappoint him. He'd taken her under his wing during high school when she and Wendy had visited the office and shown her that orthodontia was a perfect career for someone who had an obsession with making things straight and orderly.

"No *buts*." She loaded her voice with confidence.

"That's my girl." He patted her hand. "You have no idea how happy I was when you decided to join me in this practice. There's no one but you that I'd trust to turn it over to."

His words warmed and worried her at the same. The amount of responsibility overwhelmed her, but whatever it took, she'd make sure Terry never regretted choosing her.

"I won't let you down."

Crickets serenaded Jason as he headed up the walk to Ming's front door. At nine o'clock at night, only a far-off bark disturbed the peaceful tree-lined street in the older Houston suburb. Amongst the midcentury craftsman homes, Ming's contemporary-styled house stood out. The clean lines and geometric landscaping suited the woman who lived there. Ming kept her surroundings and her life uncluttered.

He couldn't imagine how she was going to handle the sort of disorder a child would bring into her world, but after his conversation with Evan this afternoon, Jason was no longer deciding whether or not he should help his oldest friend. It was more a matter of how he was going to go about it.

Jason rang her doorbell and Muffin began to bark in warning. The entry light above him snapped on and the door flew open. Jason blinked as Ming appeared in the sudden brightness. The scent of her filled his nostrils, a sumptuous floral that made him think of making love on an exotic tropical island.

"Jason? What are you doing here?" Ming bent to catch the terrier as she charged past, but missed. "Muffin, get back here."

"I'll get her." Chasing the frisky dog gave him something to concentrate on besides Ming's slender form clad in a plum silk nightgown and robe, her long black hair cascading over one shoulder. "Did I wake you?" he asked, handing her the squirming Yorkie.

His body tightened as he imagined her warm, pliant form snuggled beside him in bed. His brother had been a complete idiot not to give her the sun, moon and whatever stars she wanted.

"No." She tilted her head. "Do you want to come in?"

Swept by the new and unsettling yearning to take her in his arms and claim her lush mouth, Jason shook his head. "I've been thinking about what we talked about earlier today."

"If you've come here to talk me out of having a baby, you can save your breath." She was his best friend. Back in high school they'd agreed that what had happened after prom had been a huge mistake. They'd both been upset with their dates and turned to each other in a moment of weakness. Neither one wanted to risk their friendship by exploring the chemistry between them.

But in the back of Jason's mind, lying in wait all these years, was curiosity. What would it be like between them? It's why he'd decided to help her make a baby. Today she'd offered him the solution to satisfy his need for her and not complicate their friendship with romantic misunderstandings. He'd be a fool not to take advantage of the opportunity.

"I want to help."

"You do?" Doubt dominated her question, but relief hovered nearby. She studied him a long moment before asking, "Are you sure?"

"I've been thinking about it all afternoon and decided I'd be a pretty lousy friend if I wasn't there when you needed me."

A broad smile transformed her expression. "You don't know how much this means to me. I'll call the clinic tomorrow and make an appointment for you."

Jason shook his head. "No fertility clinic. No doctor." He hooked his fingers around the sash that held her robe closed and tugged her a half step closer. Heat pooled below his belt at the way her lips parted in surprise. "Just you and me."

Something like excitement flickered in her eyes, only to be dampened by her frown. "Are you suggesting what I think you're suggesting?"

"Let's make a baby the old-fashioned way."

Three

"Old-fashioned way?" Ming's brain sputtered like a poorly maintained engine. What the hell was he…? "Sex?"

"I prefer to think of it as making love."

"Same difference."

Jason's grin grew wolfish. "Not the way I do it."

Her mind raced. She couldn't have sex—make love—with Jason. He was her best friend. Their relationship worked because they didn't complicate it by pretending a friends-with-benefits scenario was realistic. "Absolutely not."

"Why not?"

"Because…" What was she supposed to give him for an excuse? "I don't feel that way about you."

"Give me an hour and I'm sure you'll feel exactly that way about me."

The sensual light in his eyes was so intense she could almost feel his hands sliding over her. Her nipples tightened. She crossed her arms over her chest to conceal her body's involuntary reaction.

"Arrogant jackass."

His cocky grin was her only reply. Ming scowled at him to conceal her rising alarm. He was enjoying this. Damn him. Worse, her toes were curling at the prospect of making love with him.

"Be reasonable." *Please be reasonable.* "It'll be much easier if you just go to the clinic. All you have to do is show up, grab a magazine and make a donation."

"Not happening."

The air around them crackled with electricity, raising the hair at the back of her neck.

"Why not?" She gathered the hair hanging over her shoulder and tugged. Her scalp burned at the harsh punishment. "It's not as if you have any use for them." She pointed downward.

"If you want them, you're going to have to get them the old-fashioned way."

"Stop saying that." Her voice had taken on a disturbing squeak.

Jason naked. Her hands roaming over all his hard muscles. The slide of him between her thighs. She pressed her knees together as an ache built.

"Come on," he coaxed. "Aren't you the least bit curious?"

Of course she was curious. During the months following senior prom, it's all she'd thought about. "Absolutely not."

"All the women I've dated. Haven't you wondered why they kept coming back for more?"

Instead of being turned off by his arrogance, she found his confidence arousing. "It never crossed my mind."

"I don't believe that. Not after the way you came on to me after prom."

"I came on to you? You kissed me."

"Because you batted those long black eyelashes of yours and went on and on about how no one would ever love you and how what's-his-name wasn't a real man and that you needed a real man."

Ming's mouth fell open. "I did no such thing. You were the one who put your arm around me and said the best way to get over Kevin was to get busy with someone else."

"No." He shook his head. "That's not how it happened at all."

Damn him. He'd given his word they'd never speak of it again. What other promises would he break?

"Neither one of us is going to admit we started it, so let's just agree that a kiss happened and we were prevented from making a huge mistake by my sister's phone call."

"In the interests of keeping you happy," he said, his tone sly and patronizing, "I'll agree a kiss happened and we were interrupted by your sister."

"And that afterward we both agreed it was a huge mistake."

"It was a mistake because you'd been dumped and I was fighting with my girlfriend. Neither one of us was thinking clearly."

Had she said that, or had he? The events of the night were blurry. In fact, the only thing she remembered with crystal clarity was the feel of his lips on hers. The way her head spun as he plunged his tongue into her mouth and set her afire.

"It was a mistake because we were best friends and hooking up would have messed up our relationship."

"But we're not hormone-driven teenagers anymore," he reminded her. "We can approach the sex as a naked hug between friends."

"A naked hug?" She wasn't sure whether to laugh or hit him.

What he wanted from her threatened to turn her emotions into a Gordian knot, and yet she found herself wondering if she could do as he asked. If she went into it without expectations, maybe it was possible for her to enjoy a few glorious nights in Jason's bed and get away with her head clear and her heart unharmed.

"Having…" She cleared her throat and tried again. "Making…" Her throat closed up. Completing the sentence made the prospect so much more real. She wasn't ready to go there yet.

Jason took pity on her inability to finish her thought. "Love?"

"It's intimate and…" Her skin tingled at the thought of just how intimate.

"You don't think I know that?"

Jason's velvet voice slid against her senses. Her entire body flushed as desire pulsed hot and insistent. How many times since her engagement ended had she awakened from a salacious dream about him, feeling like this? Heavy with need and too frustrated to go back to sleep? Too many nights to count.

"Let me finish," she said. "We know each other too well. We're too comfortable. There's no romance between us. It would be like brushing each other's teeth."

"Brushing each other's teeth?" he echoed, laughter dancing in his voice. "You underestimate my powers of seduction."

The wicked light in his eye promised that he was not going to be deterred from his request. A tremor threatened to upend the small amount of her confidence still standing.

"You overestimate my ability to take you seriously."

All at once he stopped trying to push her buttons and his humor faded. "If you are going to become a mother, you don't want that to happen in the sterile environment of a doctor's office. Your conception should be memorable."

She wasn't looking for memorable. Memorable lasted. It clogged up her emotions and made her long for impossible things. She wanted clinical. Practical. Uncomplicated.

Which is why her decision to ask him to be her child's father made so little sense. What if her son or daughter inherited his habit of mixing his food together on the plate before eating because he liked the way it all tasted together? That drove her crazy. She hated it when the different types of food touched each other.

Would her baby be cursed by his carefree nature and impulsiveness? His love of danger and enthusiasm for risk taking?

Or blessed with his flirtatious grin, overpowering charisma, leadership skills and athletic ability.

For someone who thought everything through, it now occurred to her that she'd settled too fast on Jason for her baby's father. As much as she'd insisted that he wouldn't be tied either legally or financially to the child, she hadn't considered how her child would be part of him.

"I would prefer my conception to be fast and efficient," she countered.

"Why not start off slow and explore where it takes us?"

Slow?

Explore?

Ming's tongue went numb. Her emotions simmered in a pot of anticipation and anxiety.

"I'm going to need to think about it."

"Take your time." If he was disappointed by her indecisiveness, he gave no indication. "I'm not going anywhere."

Three days passed without any contact from Ming. Was she considering his proposal or had she rejected the idea and was too angry at his presumption to speak to him? He shouldn't care what she chose. Either she said yes and he could have the opportunity to satisfy his craving for her, or she would refuse and he'd get over the fantasy of her moaning beneath him.

"Jason? Jason?" Max's shoulder punch brought Jason back to the racetrack. "Geez, man, where the hell's your head today?"

Cars streaked by, their powerful engines drowning out his unsettling thoughts. It was Saturday afternoon. He and Max were due to race in an hour. Driving distracted at over a hundred miles an hour was a recipe for trouble.

"Got something I didn't resolve this week."

"It's not like you to worry about work with the smell of gasoline and hot rubber on the wind."

Max's good-natured ribbing annoyed Jason as much as his

slow time in the qualifying round. Or maybe more so because it wasn't work that preoccupied Jason, but a woman.

"Yeah, well, it's a pretty big something."

Never in his life had he let a female take his mind off the business at hand. Especially when he was so determined to win this year's overall points trophy and show Max what he was missing by falling in love and getting engaged.

"Let me guess, you think someone's embezzling from Sterling Bridge."

"Hardly." As CFO of the company his grandfather began in the mid-fifties, Jason had an eagle eye for any discrepancies in the financials. "Let's just say I've put in an offer and I'm waiting to hear if it's been accepted."

"Let me guess, that '68 Shelby you were lusting after last month?"

"I'm not talking about it," Jason retorted. Let Max think he was preoccupied with a car. He'd promised Ming that he'd keep quiet about fathering her child. Granted, she hadn't agreed to let him father the child the way he wanted to, but he sensed she'd come around. It was only a matter of when.

"If it's the Shelby then it's already too late. I bought it two days ago." Max grinned at Jason's disgruntled frown. "I had a space in my garage that needed to be filled."

"And whose fault is that?" Jason spoke with more hostility than he meant to.

A couple of months ago Jason had shared with Max his theory that the Lansing Employment Agency was not in the business of placing personal assistants with executives, but in matchmaking. Max thought that was crazy. So he wagered his rare '69 'Cuda that he wouldn't marry the temporary assistant the employment agency sent him. But when the owner of the placement company turned out to be the long-lost love of Max's life, Jason gained a car but lost his best buddy.

"Why are you still so angry about winning the bet?" Despite his complaint, Max wore a good-natured grin. Everything about Max was good-natured these days. "You got the car I spent five years convincing a guy to sell me. I love that car."

He loved his beautiful fiancée more.

"I'm not angry," Jason grumbled. He missed his cynical-about-love friend. The guy who understood and agreed that love and marriage were to be avoided because falling head over heels for a woman was dangerous and risky.

"Rachel thinks you feel abandoned. Like because she and I are together, you've lost your best friend."

Jason shot Max a skeptical look. "Ming's my best friend. You're just some guy I used to hang out with before you got all stupid about a girl."

Max acted as if he hadn't heard Jason's dig. "I think she's right."

"Of course you do," Jason grumbled, pulling his ball cap off and swiping at the sweat on his forehead. "You've become one of those guys who keeps his woman happy by agreeing with everything she says."

Max smirked. "That's not how I keep Rachel happy."

For a second Jason felt a stab of envy so acute he almost winced. Silent curses filled his head as he shoved the sensation away. He had no reason to resent his friend's happiness. Max was going to spend the rest of his life devoted to a woman who might someday leave him and take his happiness with her.

"What happened to you?"

Max looked surprised by the question. "I fell in love."

"I know that." But how had he let that happen? They'd both sworn they were never going to let any woman in. After the way Max's dad cheated on his wife, Max swore he'd never trust anyone enough to fall in love. "I don't get why."

"I'd rather be with Rachel than without her."

How similar was that to what had gone through his father's mind after he'd lost his wife? His parents were best friends. Soul mates. Every cliché in the book. She was everything to him. Jason paused for breath. It had almost killed his dad to lose her.

"What if she leaves you?"

"She won't."

"What if something bad happens to her?"

"This is about what happened to your mom, isn't it?" Max gave his friend a sympathetic smile. "Being in love doesn't guarantee you'll get hurt."

"Maybe not." Jason found no glimmers of light in the shadows around his heart. "But staying single guarantees that I won't."

A week went by before Ming responded to Jason's offer to get her pregnant. She'd spent the seven days wondering what had prompted him to suggest they have sex—she just couldn't think of it as making love—and analyzing her emotional response.

Jason wasn't interested in complicating their friendship with romance any more than she was. He was the one person in her life who never expected anything from her, and she returned the favor. And yet, they were always there to help and support each other. Why risk that on the chance that the chemistry between them was out-of-this-world explosive?

Of course, it had dawned on her a couple of days ago that he'd probably decided helping her get pregnant offered him a free pass. He could get her into bed no strings attached. No worries that expectations about where things might go in the future would churn up emotions.

It would be an interlude. A couple of passionate encounters that would satisfy both their curiosities. In the end, she would be pregnant. He would go off in search of new hearts to break, and their friendship would continue on as always.

The absolute simplicity of the plan warned Ming that she was missing something.

Jason was in his garage when Ming parked her car in his

driveway and killed the engine. She hadn't completely decided to accept his terms, but she was leaning that way. It made her more sensitive to how attractive Jason looked in faded jeans and a snug black T-shirt with a Ford Mustang logo. Wholly masculine, supremely confident. Her stomach flipped in full-out feminine appreciation as he came to meet her.

"Hey, what's up?"

Light-headed from the impact of his sexy grin, she indicated the beer in his hand. "Got one of those for me?"

"Sure."

He headed for the small, well-stocked fridge at the back of the garage, and she followed. When he bent down to pull out a bottle, her gaze locked on his perfect butt. Hammered by the urge to slide her hands over those taut curves, she knew she was going to do this. Correction. She *wanted* to do this.

"Thanks," she murmured, applying the cold bottle to one overheated cheek.

Jason watched her through narrowed eyes. "I thought you didn't drink beer anymore."

"Do you have any wine?" she countered, sipping the beer and trying not to grimace.

"No."

"Then I'm drinking beer." She prowled past racing trophies and photos of Jason and Max in one-piece driving suits. "How'd your weekend go?"

"Come upstairs and see."

Jason led the way into the house and together they ascended the staircase to Jason's second floor. He'd bought the home for investment purposes and had had it professionally decorated. The traditional furnishings weren't her taste, but they suited the home's colonial styling.

He'd taken one of the four bedrooms as his man cave. A wall-to-wall tribute to his great passion for amateur car racing. On one wall, a worn leather couch, left over from his college days, sat facing a sixty-inch flat-screen TV. If Jason wasn't racing his Mustang or in the garage restoring a car, he was here, watching NASCAR events or recaps of his previous races.

He hit the play button on the remote and showed Ming the clip of the race's conclusion.

The results surprised her. "You didn't win?" He'd been having his best season ever. "What happened?"

His large frame slammed into the old couch as he sat down in a disgruntled huff. A man as competitive as Jason had a hard time coming in second. "Had a lot on my mind."

The way his gaze bore into her, Ming realized he blamed her for his loss. She joined him on the couch and jabbed her finger into his ribs. "I'm not going to apologize for taking a week to give your terms some thought."

"I would've been able to concentrate if I'd known your answer."

"I find that hard to believe," she said, keeping her tone light. Mouth Sahara dry, she drank more beer.

He dropped his arm over the back of the couch. His fingertips grazed her bare shoulder. "You don't think the thought of us making love has preoccupied me this last week?"

"Then you agree that we run the risk of changing things between us."

"It doesn't have to." Jason's fingers continued to dwell on her skin, but now he was trailing lines of fire along her collarbone. "Besides, that's not what preoccupied me."

This told Ming all she needed to know about why he'd suggested they skip the fertility clinic. For Jason this was all about the sex. Fine. It could be all about the sex for her, too.

"Okay. Let's do it." She spoke the words before she could second-guess herself. She stared at the television screen. It would be easier to say this next part without meeting his penetrating gaze. "But I have a few conditions of my own."

He leaned close enough for her to feel his breath on her neck. "You want me to romance you?"

As goose bumps appeared on her arms, she made herself

laugh. "Hardly. There is a window of three days during which we can try. If I don't get pregnant your way, then you agree to do it my way." Stipulating her terms put her back on solid ground with him. "I'm not planning on dragging this out indefinitely."

"I agree to those three days, but I want uninterrupted time with you."

She dug her fingernails beneath the beer label. In typical Jason fashion, he was messing up her well-laid plans.

She'd been thinking in terms of three short evenings of fantastic sex here at his house and then heading back home to relive the moments in the privacy of her bedroom. Not days and nights of all Jason all the time. What if she talked in her sleep and told him all her secret fantasies about him? What if he didn't let her sleep and she grew so delirious from all the hours of making love that she said something in the heat of passion?

"You're crazy if you think our families are going to leave us alone for three days."

"They will if we're not in Houston."

This was her baby. She should be the one who decided where and when it was conceived. The lack of control was making her edgy. Vulnerable.

"I propose we go somewhere far away," he continued. "A secluded spot where we can concentrate on the business at hand."

The business at hand? He caressed those four words with such a high degree of sensuality, her body vibrated with excitement.

"I'll figure out where and let you know." At least if she took charge of where they went she wouldn't have to worry about her baby being conceived in whatever town NASCAR was racing that weekend.

She started to shift her weight forward, preparing to stand, when Jason's hand slid across her abdomen and circled around to her spine.

"Before you go."

He tugged her upper half toward him. The hand that had been skimming her shoulder now cupped the back of her head. She was trapped between the heat of his body and his strong arm, her breasts skimming his chest, nipples turning into buds as desire plunged her into a whirlpool of longing. The intent in his eyes set her heart to thumping in an irregular rhythm.

"What do you think you're doing?" she demanded, retreating from the lips dipping toward hers.

"Sealing our deal with a kiss."

"A handshake will work fine."

Her brusque dismissal didn't dim the smug smile curving his lips. She put her hand on his chest. Rock-hard pecs flexed beneath her fingers. The even thump of his heart mocked her wildly fluctuating pulse.

"Not for me." He captured and held her gaze before letting his mouth graze hers. With a brief survey of her expression, he nodded. "See, that wasn't so bad."

"Right." Her chest rose and fell, betraying her agitation. "Not bad."

"If you relax it will get even better." He shifted his attention to her chin, the line of her jaw, dusting his lips over her skin and making her senses whirl.

"I'm not ready to relax." She'd geared up to tell him that she'd try getting pregnant his way. Getting physical with him would require a different sort of preparation.

"You don't have to get ready." His chest vibrated with a low chuckle. "Just relax."

"Jason, how long have we known each other?"

"Long time." He found a spot that interested him just below her ear and lingered until she shivered. "Why?"

Her voice lacked serenity as she said, "Then you know I don't do anything without planning."

His exhalation tickled her sensitive skin and made holding still almost impossible. "You don't need to plan. Just let go."

Right. And risk him discovering her secret? Ever since she'd decided to ask his help in getting pregnant, she'd realized that what she felt for him was deeper than friendship. Not love. Or not the romantic sort. At least she didn't think so. Not yet. But it could become that sort of love if they made love over and over and over.

And if he found out how her feelings had changed toward him, he'd bolt the way he'd run from every other woman who'd tried to claim his heart.

Ming tensed to keep from responding to the persuasive magic of his touch. Just the sweep of his lips over her skin, the strength of his arms around her, raised her temperature and made her long for him to take her hard and fast.

"I'll let go when we're out of town," she promised. Well, lied really. At least she hoped she was lying. "What are you doing?"

In a quick, powerful move, he'd shifted her onto her back and slid one muscular leg between her thighs. Her body reacted before her mind caught up. She bent her knees, planted her feet on the couch cushions and rocked her hips in the carnal hope of easing the ache in her loins.

"While you make arrangements for us to go away, I thought you'd feel better if you weren't worried about the chemistry between us."

His heat seeped into her, softening her muscles, reducing her resistance to ash. "No worries here. I'm sure you're a fabulous lover." She trembled in anticipation of just how fabulous. With her body betraying her at his every touch, she had to keep her wits sharp. "Otherwise, why else would you have left a trail of broken hearts in your wake?"

Jason frowned. "I didn't realize that bothered you so much."

"It doesn't."

He hummed his doubt and leaned down to nibble on her earlobe. "Not sure I believe you."

With her erogenous zones on full red alert, she labored to keep her legs from wrapping around his hips. She wanted to feel him hard and thick against the thudding ache between her thighs. Her fingernails dug into the couch cushions.

"You're biting your lip." His tongue flicked over the tender spot. "I don't know why you're fighting this so hard."

And she didn't want him to find out. "Okay. I'm not worried about your sexual prowess. I'm worried that once we go down this path, there'll be no turning back."

"Oh, I see. You're worried you're going to fall in love with me."

"No." She made a whole series of disgruntled, dismissive noises until she realized he was teasing her. Two could play at this game. "I'm more concerned you'll fall in love with me."

"I don't think that's going to happen."

"I don't know," she said, happy to be on the giving end of the ribbing. "I'm pretty adorable."

"That you are." He scanned her face, utterly serious. "Close your eyes," he commanded. "We're going to do this."

She complied, hoping the intimacy they shared as friends would allow her to revel in the passion Jason aroused in her and keep her from worrying about the potential complications. Being unable to see Jason's face helped calm the flutters of anxiety. If she ignored the scent of sandalwood mingled with car polish, she might be able to pretend the man lying on top of her was anyone else.

The sound of his soft exhalation drifted past her ears a second before his lips found hers. Ming expected him to claim her mouth the way he had fifteen years ago and kiss her as if she was the only woman in the world he'd ever wanted. But this kiss was different. It wasn't the wild, exciting variety that had caused her to tear at Jason's shirt and allow him to slip his hand down the bodice of her dress to bare her breasts.

Jason's lips explored hers with firm but gentle pressure. If she'd worried that she'd be overcome with desire and make a complete fool of herself over him, she'd wasted her energy.

This kiss was so controlled and deliberate she wondered if Jason was regretting his offer to make love to her.

An empty feeling settled in her chest.

"See," Jason said, drifting his lips over her eyelids. "That wasn't so bad."

"I never expected it would be."

"Then what are you so afraid of?"

What if her lust for him was stronger than his for her? What if three days with him only whet her appetite for more?

"The thought of you seeing me naked is one," she said, keeping her tone light to hide her dismay.

His grin bloomed, mischievous and naughty. "I've already seen you naked."

"What?" Lust shot through Ming, leaving her dazzled and disturbed. "When?"

"Remember that family vacation when we brought you with us to Saint John? The outdoor shower attached to my bedroom?"

"Everyone was snorkeling. That's why I came back to the villa early." She'd wanted the room Jason ended up with because of the outdoor shower. Thinking she was alone, she'd used it. "You spied on me?"

"More like stumbled upon you."

She shoved at his beefy shoulder but couldn't budge him. "Why did you have to tell me that?"

"To explain why you have no need to be embarrassed. I've seen it all before." And from his expression, he'd liked what he saw.

Ming flushed hot. Swooning was impossible if she was lying down, right?

"How long did you watch me?"

"Five, maybe ten minutes."

Her mouth opened, but no words came out. Goose bumps erupted at the way his gaze trailed over her. Was she wrong about the kiss? Or was she the only one who caught fire every time they touched?

He stood and offered her his hand. She let him pull her to her feet and then set about straightening her clothes and finger-combing her hair.

Already she could feel their friendship morphing into something else. By the time their three days together were up, she would no longer be just his friend. She would be his ex-lover. That would alter her perspective of their relationship. Is that really what she wanted?

"I've been charting my cycle for the last six months," she said, uncaring if he'd be disinterested in her feminine activities. "The next time I ovulate is in ten days. Can you get away then?"

"Are you sure you want to go through with this?"

Had he hoped his kiss would change her mind? "I really want this baby. If sleeping with you is the only way that's going to happen, I'm ready to make the sacrifice."

He grinned. "Make the arrangements."

Four

Ming had chosen Mendocino, California, for her long weekend with Jason because the only person who knew it was her favorite getaway spot was Terry's daughter, Wendy, her closest girlfriend from high school. Wendy had moved to California with her husband seven years earlier and had introduced Ming to the town, knowing she would fall in love with the little slice of New England plopped onto a rugged California coast. The area featured some of the most spectacular scenery Ming had ever seen, and every year thereafter she returned for a relaxing long weekend.

That all had ended two years ago. She'd arrived early in September for a few days of spa treatments and soul-searching. Surrounded by the steady pulse of shore life, she lingered over coffee, browsed art galleries and wine shops, and took a long look at her relationship with Evan. They'd been going out for a little over a year and he'd asked her to decide between becoming a fully committed couple or parting ways.

That long weekend in Mendocino she'd decided to stop feeling torn between the Sterling brothers. She loved Evan one way. She loved Jason another. He'd been nothing but supportive of her dating Evan and more preoccupied than ever with his career and racing hobby. Ming doubted Jason had even noticed that Evan took up most of her time and attention. Or maybe she just wished it had bothered him. That he'd tell his brother to back off and claim Ming as his own.

But he hadn't, and it had nagged at her how easily Jason had let her go. She'd not viewed a single one of his girlfriends as casually. Each new love interest had meant Jason had taken his friendship with Ming even more for granted.

In hindsight, she understood how she'd fallen for Evan. He'd showered her with all the attention she could ever want.

Despite how things worked out between them, she'd never regretted dating Evan or agreeing to be his wife. So what if their relationship lacked the all-consuming passion of a romance novel. They'd respected each other, communicated logically and without drama. They'd enjoyed the same activities and possessed similar temperaments. All in all, Evan made complete sense for her as a life partner. But had everything been as perfect as it seemed?

A hundred times in the past six months she'd questioned whether she'd have gone through with the wedding if Evan hadn't changed his mind about having kids and ended their engagement.

They'd dated for two years, been engaged for one.

Plenty of time to shake off doubts about the future.

Plenty of time to decide if what she felt for Evan was enduring love or if she'd talked herself into settling for good enough because he fit seamlessly into her picture of the perfect life.

They were ideally suited in temperament and ideology. He never challenged her opinions or bullied her into defending her beliefs. She always knew where she stood with him. He'd made her feel safe.

A stark contrast to the wildly shifting emotions Jason aroused in her.

The long drive up from San Francisco gave Ming too much time to think. To grow even more anxious about the weekend with Jason. Already plagued by concern that letting him help her conceive a baby would complicate their relationship, now she had to worry that making love with him might just whip up a frenzy of emotions that would lead her to disappointment.

Knowing full well she was stalling, Ming stopped in Mendocino and did some window-shopping before she headed to the inn where she and Jason would be staying. To avoid anyone getting suspicious about the two of them doing something as unusual as heading to California for the weekend, they'd travelled separately. Ming had flown to San Francisco a few days ago to spend some time with Wendy. Jason had headed out on Friday morning. As much as Ming enjoyed visiting with her friend, she'd been preoccupied with doubts and worries that she couldn't share.

Although Wendy was excited about Ming's decision to have a baby, she wouldn't have approved of Ming's choice of Jason as the father. So Ming kept that part of her plans to herself. Wendy had been there for all Ming's angst in the aftermath of the senior prom kiss and believed she had wasted too much energy on a man who was never going to let himself fall in love and get married.

Add to this her sister's disapproval, and the fact that the one person she'd always been able to talk to when something was eating at her was the source of her troubles, and Ming was drowning in uncertainty.

The sun was inching its way toward the horizon when Ming decided she'd dawdled long enough. She paid the gallery owner for the painting of the coast she'd fallen in love with and made arrangements to have it shipped back to her house. Her feet felt encased in lead as she headed down the steps toward her rental car.

She drove below the speed limit on the way to the inn. Gulls wheeled and dove in the steady winds off the Pacific as the car rolled down the driveway, gravel crunching beneath the tires. Silver Mist Inn was composed of a large central lodge and a collection of small cottages that clung to the edge of the cliffs. The spectacular views were well matched by the incredible cuisine and the fabulous hospitality of the husband-and-wife team who owned the inn and spa.

Rosemary was behind the check-in desk when Ming entered the lodge. "Hello, Ming," the fifty-something woman exclaimed. "How wonderful to see you."

Ming smiled. Already the relaxing, familiar feel of the place was sinking into her bones. "It's great to see you, too, Rosemary. How have you been?"

Her gaze drifted to the right of reception. The lodge's main room held a handful of people sipping coffee, reading or talking while they enjoyed the expansive views of the ocean. Off to the left, a door led to a broad deck that housed lounge chairs where waitresses were busy bringing drinks from the bar.

"Busy as always." Rosemary pushed a key toward Ming. "Your friend checked in three hours ago. You're staying in Blackberry Cottage."

The change of plans revived Ming's earlier uneasiness. "I booked my regular room in the lodge."

Rosemary nodded. "After your friend saw all we had to offer, he wanted to upgrade your accommodations. It's a little bigger, way more private and the views are the best we have."

"Thank you." Ming forced her lips into a smile she wasn't feeling.

Why had Jason disrupted her arrangements? Whenever she vacationed here, she always stayed in the same room, a comfortable suite with a large balcony that overlooked the ocean. This weekend in particular she'd wanted to be in familiar surroundings.

Ming parked her car beside the one Jason had rented and

retrieved her overnight bag from the trunk. Packing had taken her three hours. She'd debated every item that had gone into the carry-on luggage.

What sort of clothes would set the correct tone for the weekend? She'd started with too much outerwear. But the purpose of the trip wasn't to wander the trails by the cliffs but to explore Jason's glorious, naked body.

So, she'd packed the sexy lingerie she'd received as a bridal shower gift but never gotten the chance to wear. As she'd folded the silky bits of lace and satin, she realized the provocative underwear sent a message that Ming hoped to drive Jason wild with passion, and that struck her as very nonfriendlike.

In the end, she'd filled the suitcase with leggings and sweaters to combat the cool ocean breezes and everyday lingerie because she was making too big a deal out of what was to come.

Ming entered the cottage and set her suitcase by the front door. Her senses purred as she gazed around the large living room decorated in soothing blues and golds. Beyond the cozy furnishings was a wall of windows that revealed a deck gilded by the setting sun and beyond, the indigo ocean.

To her right something mouthwatering was cooking in the small, well-appointed kitchen. An open door beside the refrigerator led outside. Nearing the kitchen, she spied Jason enjoying the ocean breezes from one of the comfortable chairs that flanked a love seat on the deck.

For an undisturbed moment she observed him. He was as relaxed as she'd seen him in months, expression calm, shoulders loose, hands at ease on the chair's arms. A sharp stab of anticipation made her stomach clench. Shocked by the excitement that flooded her, Ming closed her eyes and tried to even out her breathing. In a few short hours, maybe less, they would make love for the first time. Her skin prickled, flushed. Heat throbbed through her, forging a path that ended between her thighs.

Panic followed. She wasn't ready for this. For him.

Telling her frantic pulse to calm down, Ming stepped onto the deck. "Hi."

Jason's gaze swung her way. A smile bloomed. "Hi yourself." He stood and stepped toward her. "You're later than I expected."

His deep voice and the intense light in his eyes made her long to press herself into his arms and pretend they were a real couple and that this was a magical getaway. She dug her nails into her palms.

"It's been over a year since I've seen Wendy. We had a lot to catch up on."

"What was her take on your decision to have a baby?"

"Total support." Ming slipped past him and leaned her elbows on the railing. As the sapphire-blue ocean churned against rugged cliffs, sending plumes of water ten feet into the air, she put her face into the breeze and let it cool her hot cheeks. "After the week I had, it was a relief to tell someone who didn't go all negative on me."

"I wasn't negative."

Ming tore her gaze from the panorama and discovered Jason two feet away. Attacked by delicious tingles, she shook her head. "No, but you created trouble for me, nonetheless."

"Did you tell her about us?"

Ming shook her head. "We're supposed to keep this a secret, remember? Besides, she never liked you in high school."

"Everybody liked me in high school."

Although he'd been a jock and one of the most popular guys in school, Jason hadn't been mean to those less blessed the way his football buddies had been.

"Don't you mean all the girls?" Blaming nerves for her disgruntled tone, Ming pressed her lips together and redirected her attention to the view. The sun was still too bright to stare at, but the color was changing rapidly to orange.

"Them, too." Jason reached out and wrapped the ends of her scarf around his fists.

He tugged, startling her off balance, and stepped into her space. Her hormones shrieked in delight as the scent of cologne and predatory male surrounded her. She gulped air into her lungs and felt her breasts graze his chest. A glint appeared in his eyes, sending a spike of excitement through her.

"Something smells great in the kitchen. What's for dinner?" she asked, her voice cracking on the last word. Her appetite had vanished in the first rush of desire, but eating would delay what came later.

"Coq au vin." Although his lips wore a playful smile, his preoccupation with her mouth gave the horseplay a sexual vibe. He looked prepared to devour her in slow, succulent bites. "Your favorite. Are you hungry?"

He looked half-starved.

"I haven't eaten since breakfast." Her stomach had been too knotted to accept food.

"Then I'd better feed you." He softened his fists and let her scarf slip through his fingers, releasing her. "You'll need your strength for what I have planned for you tonight."

Freed, Ming couldn't move. The hunger prowling through her prevented her from backing to a safe distance. His knowing smirk kept her tongue-tied. She silently cursed as she trailed after him into the kitchen.

"I found a really nice chardonnay in town." He poured two glasses of wine and handed one to Ming. "I figured we'd save the champagne for later."

Great. He was planning to get her liquored up. She could blame the alcohol for whatever foolish thing she cried out in the heat of passion. She swallowed half the pale white wine in a single gulp and made approving noises while he pulled a wedge of brie out of the fridge. Grapes. Crackers. Some sort of pâté. All the sort of thing she'd served him at some point. Had he paid attention to what she liked? Asking herself the question had an adverse effect on her knees and led to more dangerous ruminating. What else might he have planned for her?

"Dinner should be ready in half an hour." He had everything assembled on a plate and used his chin to gesture toward the deck. "It's a gorgeous night. Let's not waste the good weather."

Early September in northern California was a lot cooler than what they'd left behind in Houston, and Ming welcomed the break from the heat. "It really is beautiful." She carried their glasses outside. "We should take a long walk after dinner."

Jason set down the plate and shot her a look. "If you have any strength in your legs after I'm done with you, we'll do that."

Despite the hot glance that accompanied his suggestive words, she shivered. Is this how the weekend was going to go? One long flirtation? It took them away from their normal interaction. Made her feel as if they'd grown apart these past few years and lost the comfortable intimacy they'd once shared.

"You're cold. Come sit with me and I'll warm you up."

Her scattered wits needed time to recover before she was ready to have his arms around her. "I'll grab my wrap."

"Let me get it."

"It's on my suitcase by the door."

How was she supposed to resist falling under his spell if he continued being so solicitous? This was the Jason she'd glimpsed with other women. The one she'd longed to have for her own. Only this Jason never stayed to charm any one woman for more than a few months, while Ming had enjoyed her fun-loving, often self-involved friend in her life for over twenty years. She sighed. Was it possible for him to be the thoughtful, romantic lover and a great friend all in one?

Was she about to find out? Or would making love with him complicate her life? Was he close to discovering she'd harbored a secret, unrequited crush on him for years? At best he'd not take it seriously and tease her about it. At worst, he'd put up walls and disappear the way he always did when a girlfriend grew too serious. Either way, she wasn't ready for his pity or his alarm.

Jason returned with her dark blue pashmina. "I put your suitcase in the bedroom."

Foolishly her heart jerked at the last word. Every instinct told her to run. Altering their relationship by becoming sexually intimate was only going to create problems.

Then he was wrapping the shawl around her and grazing her lips with his. All thoughts of fleeing vanished, lost in the heat generated by her frantic heart.

She put a hand on his arm. "Jason—"

He put a finger against her lips and silenced her. "Save it for later."

The twinkle in his eye calmed some of the frenzy afflicting her hormones. She reminded herself that he was way more experienced in the art of seduction, having had vast numbers of willing women to practice on. He liked the chase. It was routine that turned him off. And right now, he was having a ball pursuing her. Maybe if she stopped resisting, he'd turn down the charisma.

So, she took half a dozen slow, deep breaths and forced herself to relax. Nibbling cheese, she stared at their view and kept her gaze off the handsome man with the dazzling blue eyes. But his deep voice worked its way inside her, its rumble shaking loose her defenses. She let him feed her grapes and crackers covered with pâté. His fingers skimmed her lips, dusted sensation over her cheeks and chin. By the time they were bumping hips in the small kitchen while transferring coq au vin and potatoes to plates, pouring more wine and assembling cutlery, Ming had gotten past her early nerves.

This was the Jason she adored. Funny, completely present, a tad bit naughty. The atmosphere between them was as easy as it had ever been. They'd discussed Terry's offer to take over the practice. Her sister's decision to buy a house in Portland. And stayed away from the worrisome topic of what was going to happen after dessert.

"This is delicious," Ming murmured, closing her eyes in

rapture as the first bite of coq au vin exploded on her taste buds. "My favorite."

"I thought you'd appreciate it. Rosemary told me the restaurant was known for their French cuisine." Jason had yet to sample the dinner.

She indicated his untouched plate. "Aren't you hungry?" He sure looked half-starved.

"I'm having too much fun watching you eat."

And just like that the sizzle was back in the room. Ming's mouth went dry. She bypassed her wine and sipped water instead. After her first glass of the chardonnay, she'd barely touched her second. Making love to Jason for the first time demanded a clear head. She wanted to be completely in the moment, not lost in an alcoholic fog.

"How can watching me eat be fun?" She tried to make her tone light and amused, but it came out husky and broken.

"It's the pleasure you take in each bite. The way you savor the flavors. You're usually so matter-of-fact about things, I like knowing what turns you on."

He wasn't talking about food. Ming felt her skin heat. Her blood moved sluggishly through her veins. Even her heart seemed to slow. She could feel a sexy retort forming on her tongue. She bit down until she had it restrained. They were old friends who were about to have sex, not a man and a woman engaged in a romantic ritual that ended in passionate lovemaking. Ming had to be certain her emotions stayed out of the mix. She could count on Jason to do the same.

"The backs of my knees are very ticklish." She focused on cutting another bite of chicken. "I've always loved having my neck kissed. And there's a spot on my pelvis." She paused, cocked her head and tried to think about the exact spot. "I guess I'll have to show you when we get to that point." She lifted her fork and speared him with a matter-of-fact gaze. "And you?"

His expression told her he was on to her game. "I'm a guy.

Pretty much anywhere a beautiful woman touches me, I'm turned on."

"But there has to be something you really like."

His eyes narrowed. "My nipples are very sensitive."

She pressed her lips together to keep from laughing. "I'll pay special attention to them," she said when she trusted her voice.

If they could talk like this in the bedroom, Ming was confident she could emerge from the weekend without doing something remarkably stupid like mentioning how her feelings for him had been evolving over the last few months. She'd keep things casual. Focus on the physical act, not the intimacy. Use her hands, mouth and tongue to appreciate the perfection of Jason's toned, muscular body and avoid thinking about all those tiresome longings she'd bottled up over the years.

Savor the moment and ignore the future.

While Jason cleared the dishes from the table, Ming went to unpack and get ready for what was to come. Her confidence had returned over dinner. She had her priorities all in a row. Her gaze set on the prize. The path to creating a baby involved being intimate with Jason. She would let her body enjoy making love with him. Emotion had no place in what she was about to do.

Buoyed by her determination, Ming stopped dead in the doorway between the living room and bedroom. The scene before her laid waste to all her good intentions. Here was the stuff of seduction.

The centerpiece of the room was a king-size bed with the white down comforter pulled back and about a hundred red rose petals strewn across the white sheets. Candles covered every available surface, unlit but prepared to set a romantic mood when called upon. Piano music, played by her favorite artist, poured from the dresser, where portable speakers had been attached to an iPod. Everything was perfect.

Her chest locked up. She could not have designed a better setting. Jason had gone to a lot of trouble to do this. He'd planned, taken into account all her favorite things and executed all of this to give her the ideal romantic weekend.

It was so unlike him to think ahead and be so prepared. To take care of her instead of the other way around. It was as if she was here with a completely different person. A thoughtful, romantic guy who wanted something more than three days of great sex and then going back to being buddies. The sort of man women fell for and fell for hard.

"What do you think?"

She hadn't heard Jason's approach over the thump of her heart. "What I think is that I can't do this."

Jason surveyed the room, searching for imperfections. The candles were vanilla scented, her favorite. The rose petals on the bed proclaimed that this weekend was about romance rather than just sex. The coq au vin had been delicious. Everything he'd done was intended to set the perfect stage for romance.

He'd given her no indication that he intended to rush her. He'd promised her a memorable weekend. She had to know he'd take his time with her, drive her wild with desire. This wasn't some spontaneous hookup for him. He took what they were about to do seriously.

What the hell could possibly be wrong?

"I'm sorry," she said into the silence. Sagging against the door frame, she closed her eyes and the weight of the world appeared to descend on her.

"I don't understand."

"I don't, either." She looked beautiful and tragic as she opened her eyes and met his gaze. "I want to do this."

He was very glad to hear that because anticipation had been eating him alive these past few days. He wanted her with an intensity he'd never felt before. Maybe that was because ever since he'd kissed her, he'd been fantasizing about this moment. Or maybe he'd never worked this hard to get a woman into bed before.

"Being a mom is all I think about these days. I know if I want your help to get pregnant, we have to do it this weekend." Ming lapsed into silence, her hunched shoulders broadcasting discomfort.

"I didn't realize making love with me required so much sacrifice on your part." He forced amusement into his tone to keep disappointment at bay.

Her words had cut deep. When he'd insisted they make her baby this way instead of going to a clinic, he thought this would be the perfect opportunity to satisfy his longing for her. The kiss between them a few days earlier confirmed the attraction between them was mutual. Why was she resisting when the vibe between them was electric? What was she afraid of?

"I didn't mean it that way." But from her unhappy expression his accusation hadn't been far off.

"No?" Jason leaned against the wall and fought the urge to snatch her into his arms and kiss her senseless. He could seduce her, but he didn't want just her body, he wanted... "How exactly did you mean it?"

"Look, we're best friends. Don't you think sleeping together will make things awkward between us?"

"Not possible. It's because we're just friends that it will work so great." He sounded as if he was overselling used cars of dubious origin. "No expectations—"

"No strings?"

He didn't like the way she said that. As if he'd just confirmed her worst fears. "Are you worried that I'm in this just for the sex?" She wasn't acting as if she hoped it would lead to something more.

"Yes." She frowned, clearly battling conflicting opinions. "No."

"But you have some sort of expectation." Jason was surprised that his flight response wasn't stimulated by her question. Usually when a woman started thinking too much, it was time to get out.

"Not the sort you mean." She gave her head a vigorous shake. "I know perfectly well that once we have sex—"

"Make love."

"Whatever." She waved her hand as if she was batting away a pesky fly. "That once we…become intimate, you will have your curiosity satisfied—"

"Curiosity?" The word exploded from him. That's not how he'd describe the hunger pulsing through him. "You think all I feel is curiosity?"

She gave him a little shoulder shrug. Frustration clawed at him. The bed was feet away. He was damned tempted to scoop her up in his arms and drop her onto the softly scented sheets. Give her a taste of exactly what he was feeling.

He pushed off the wall and let his acute disappointment and eight-inch height advantage intimidate her into taking a step back. "And what about you? Aren't you the least bit curious how hot this thing between us will burn?"

"Oh, please. I'm not one of the women you date."

The second she rolled her eyes at him, Jason knew he'd hit a soft spot. Ming overthought everything. She liked her life neat and orderly. That was great for her career, but in her personal life she could use a man who overwhelmed her senses and short-circuited her thoughts. His brother hadn't been able to do it. Evan had once complained that his fiancée had a hard time being spontaneous and letting go. He'd never come right out and said that she'd been reserved in bed. Evan had too much respect for Ming to be so crass, but Jason had been able to read between the lines.

"What is that supposed to mean?"

"Has it ever occurred to you to look at the sort of women you prefer to date?"

"Beautiful. Smart. Sexy."

"Needy. Clinging. Terrified of abandonment." She crossed her arms over her chest and stared him down as no one else did. "You choose needy women to get your ego stroked and then, when you start to pull away because they're too clingy, they fear your abandonment and chase you."

"That's ridiculous." Jason wasn't loving the picture she was painting of him. Nor was this conversation creating the romantic mood he'd hoped for, but he refused to drop the subject until he'd answered her charges.

"Jennifer was a doctor," he said, listing the last three women he'd dated. "Amanda owned a very successful boutique and Sherri was a vice president of marketing. Independent, successful women all."

"Jennifer had daddy issues." She ticked the women off on her fingers. "Her father was a famous cardiologist and never let her feel as if she was good enough even though she finished second in her class at med school. Amanda was a middle child. She had four brothers and sisters and never felt as if her parents had time for her. As for Sherri, her mom left when she was seven. She had abandonment issues."

"How did you know all that?"

Ming's long-suffering look made his gut tighten. "Who do you think they come to when the relationship starts to cool?"

"What do you tell them?"

"That as wonderful as you are, any relationship with you has little chance of becoming permanent. You are a confirmed bachelor and an adrenaline junky with an all-consuming hobby who will eventually break their heart."

"Do they listen to you?"

"The healthy ones do."

"You know, if we weren't such old and dear friends, I might be tempted to take offense."

"You won't," she said confidently. "Because deep down you know you choose damaged women so eventually their issues will cause trouble between you and you have the perfect excuse to break things off."

Deep down he knew this? "And here I thought I dated them because they were hot." About then, Jason realized Ming had picked a fight with him. "I don't want to talk about all the women I've dated." But it was too late.

Ming wore the mulish expression he'd first encountered on the playground when one of his buddies had shoved her off the swings.

"This weekend was a mistake." She slipped sideways into the bedroom and headed straight for her suitcase.

To Jason's bafflement, she used it as a battering ram, clearing him from her path to the front door.

"You're leaving?"

"You thought conceiving a baby should be memorable, but the only thing I'm going to remember about being here with you is this fight."

"We're not fighting." She was making no sense, and Jason wasn't sure how trying to provide her with a romantic setting for their first time together had sparked her wrath. "Where do you think you're going?"

"Back to San Francisco. There's a midnight flight that will put me back in Houston by morning."

How could she know that unless…? "You'd already decided you weren't going to stay."

"Don't be ridiculous." Her voice rang with sincerity, but she was already out the door and her face was turned away from him. "I just happened to notice it when I was booking my flight."

Ming was approaching the trunk of her rental car as Jason barreled through the front door and halted. His instincts told him to stop her. He was reasonably certain he could coax her mood back to romance with her favorite dessert and a stroll through the gardens, but her words had him wondering about his past choices when it came to relationships.

In the deepening twilight, a full harvest moon, robust and orange from the sunset, crested the trees. A lovers' moon. Pity it would go to waste on them.

Jason dug his fingers into the door as Ming turned her car

around. Was giving her time to think a good idea? He was gambling that eventually she'd remember that she needed him to get pregnant.

Five

Ming hadn't been able to sleep on the red-eye from San Francisco to Houston. The minute her car had reached the Mendocino city limits, she'd begun to feel the full weight of her mistake. She had three choices: convince Jason to use a clinic for her conception, give up on him being her child's father or stop behaving like a ninny and have sex with him. Because it was her nature to do so, she spent the flight home making pro and con lists for each choice. Then she weighted each item and analyzed her results.

Logic told her to head for the nearest sperm bank. Instead, as soon as the wheels of the plane hit the runway, she texted him an apology and asked him to call as soon as he was able.

The cab from the airport dropped her off at nine in the morning. She entered her house and felt buffeted by its emptiness. With Lily in Portland and Muffin spending the weekend with Ming's parents, she had the place to herself. The prospect depressed her, but she was too exhausted to fetch the active Yorkshire terrier.

Closing the curtains in her room, she slid between the sheets but didn't fall asleep as soon as her head touched the pillow. She tortured herself with thoughts of making love with Jason. Imagined his strong body moving against her, igniting her passion. Her body pulsed with need. If she hadn't panicked, she wouldn't feel like a runaway freight train. She'd be sated and sleepy instead of wide awake and horny.

Ming buried her face in the pillow and screamed her frustration until her throat burned. That drained enough of her energy to allow her to sleep. She awakened some hours later, disoriented by the dark room, and checked the clock. It was almost five. She pushed to a sitting position and raked her long hair away from her face. Despite sleeping for six hours, she was far from rested. Turbulent dreams of Jason returned her to that unfulfilled state that had plagued her earlier.

If not for the evocative scents of cooking, she might have spent what remained of the day in bed, but her stomach growled, reminding her she hadn't had anything to eat except the power bar she'd bought at the airport. She got dressed and went to the kitchen to investigate.

"Something smells great." Ming stepped off the back stairs and into her kitchen, surprising her sister.

The oven door closed with a bang as she spun to face Ming. "You're home." Lily's cheeks bore a rosy flush, probably put there by whatever simmered on the stove.

Even though both girls had learned to cook from their mother, only Lily had inherited their mother's passion for food. Ming knew enough to keep from starving, but for her cooking was more of a necessity than an infatuation.

"You're cooking."

"I was craving lamb."

"Craving it?" The dish was a signature item Lily prepared when she was trying to impress a guy. It had been over a year since she'd made it. "I thought you were going to be house hunting in Portland this weekend."

"I changed my mind about spending the weekend."

"Does this mean you're changing your mind about moving?" Ming quizzed, unable to contain the hope in her voice.

"No." Lily pulled a bottle of wine from the fridge and dug in a drawer for the corkscrew. "How come you're home so early? I thought you were gone all weekend."

Ming thought of the chardonnay she and Jason had shared. How he'd fed her grapes and how she'd enjoyed his hands on her skin. "I wasn't having any fun so I thought I'd come home." Not the whole truth, but far from a lie. "I didn't get a chance to tell you before you left town last week, but Terry wants to sell me his half of the practice. He's retiring."

"How are you going to manage a baby and the practice all by yourself?"

"I can handle it just fine."

"I think you're being selfish." Lily's words, muffled by the refrigerator door, drove a spear into Ming's heart. She pulled a bowl of string beans out and plunked them on the counter. "How can you possibly have enough time for a child when you're running the practice?"

"There are a lot of professional women who manage to do both." Ming forced back the doubts creeping up on her, but on the heels of her failure with Jason this weekend, she couldn't help but wonder if her subconscious agreed with Lily.

What if she couldn't do both well? Was she risking complete failure? No. She could do this. Even without a partner in her life to help her when things went wrong, or to celebrate the triumphs?

She was going to be awfully lonely. Sure, her parents would help when they could, but Lily was moving and Jason had his racing and his career to occupy him. What was she thinking? She would have her child and the practice to occupy her full attention. What about love? Marriage?

She brushed aside the questions. What good did it do to

focus on something she couldn't control? Planning and organization led to success, and she was a master of both.

With her confidence renewed, she poured wine from the bottle Lily had opened. As it hit her taste buds, she made a face. She checked the label and frowned at her sister.

"Since when do you drink Riesling?"

"I'm trying new things."

"This is Evan's favorite wine."

"He recommended it so I bought a bottle."

"Recently?"

"No." Her sister frowned. "A while ago. Geez, what's with all the questions? I tried a type of wine your ex liked. Big deal."

Lily's sharpness rocked Ming. Was her sister so upset with her that it threatened to drive a wedge between them?

Ming set down her wineglass. "I'm going to run over to Mom and Dad's and pick up Muffin. Is there anything you need me to get while I'm out?"

"How about a bottle of wine you prefer?"

Flinching at her sister's unhappy tone, Ming grabbed her keys and headed for the door. "You know, I'm not exactly thrilled with your decision to move to Portland, but I know it's something you feel you have to do, so I'm trying to put aside my selfish wish for you to stay and at least act like I'm supportive."

Then, without waiting for her sister's reply, Ming stepped into her garage and shut the door firmly behind her. With her hands shaking, she had a hard time getting the key into the ignition of the '66 Shelby Cobra. She'd chosen to drive the convertible tonight, hoping the fresh air might clear away all the confusion in her mind.

The drive to her parents' house was accomplished in record time thanks to the smoothly purring 425 V8 engine. She really should sell the car. It was an impractical vehicle for a mother-to-be, but she had such great memories of the summer she and Jason had spent fixing it up.

After her spat with Lily, she'd planned to join her parents for dinner, but they were meeting friends at the country club, so Ming collected her dog and retraced her path back to her house. A car sat in her driveway. In the fading daylight, it took her a second to recognize it as Evan's.

Because she and Jason were best friends and she knew there'd be occasions when she'd hang out with his family, Ming had made a decision to keep her interactions with Evan amicable. In fact, it wasn't that hard. Their relationship lacked the turbulent passion that would make her hate him for dumping her. But that didn't mean she was okay about him showing up without warning.

Ming parked the convertible in the garage. Disappointment filled her as she tucked Muffin under her arm and exited the car. She'd been hoping Jason had stopped by. He hadn't called her or responded to her text.

When she entered the house, the tension in the kitchen stopped her like an invisible wall. What the heck? Evan and her sister had chosen opposite sides of the center island. An almost empty wine bottle sat between them. Lily's mouth was set in unhappy lines. Her gaze dropped from Evan to the bowl of lettuce on the counter before her.

"Evan, this is a surprise." Ming eyed the vase of flowers beside the sink. Daisies. The same big bunch he always gave her after they'd had a difference of opinion. He thought the simple white flower represented a sweet apology. He was nothing if not predictable. Or maybe not so predictable. Why had he shown up on her doorstep without calling?

Lily didn't look Ming's way. Had her sister shared with Evan her dismay about Ming's decision to have a baby? Stomach churning, she set Muffin down. The terrier headed straight for her food bowl.

"What brings you here?" Ming asked.

"I came by to… Because…" He appeared at a loss to explain his reason for visiting.

"Are you staying for dinner? Lily's making rack of lamb. I'm sure there's enough for three, or I should say four, since usually she makes it for whomever she's dating at the time."

Evan's gaze sliced toward Lily. "You're dating someone?"

"Not dating exactly, just using him for sex." Ming lowered her voice. "Although I think she's ready to find someone she can get serious about. That's why she's moving to Portland."

"And the guy she's seeing." Since Lily refused to look up from the lettuce she was shredding, Evan directed the question at Ming. "She can't get serious about him?"

"She says they're just friends." The Yorkie barked and Ming filled Muffin's bowl. "Isn't that right, Lily?"

"I guess." Lily's gaze darted between Ming and Evan.

"So, when are you expecting him to show?"

"Who?"

"The guy you're preparing the lamb for."

"There's no guy," Lily retorted, her tone impatient. "I told you I was craving lamb. No big deal."

Ming felt the touch of Evan's gaze. She'd been using Lily's love life to distract him from whatever purpose he had for visiting her tonight. Something about Evan had changed in the past year. The closer they got to their wedding, the more he'd let things irritate him. A part of her had been almost relieved when he called things off.

What was he doing here tonight? She glanced at the daisies. If he was interested in getting back together, his timing was terrible.

"I'm going to head upstairs and unpack," she told them, eager to escape. "Evan, make sure you let me know if Lily's mystery man shows up. I'm dying to meet him."

"There's no mystery man," her sister yelled up the stairs at her.

Ming set her suitcase on the bed and began pulling clothes out of it. She put everything where it belonged, hamper and dry cleaning pile for the things she'd worn, drawers and hangers for what she hadn't. When she was done, only one item remained. A white silk nightie. Something a bride might wear on her wedding night. She'd bought it in San Francisco two days ago specifically for her weekend with Jason.

Now what was she supposed to do with it?

"Ming?"

She spun around at the sound of Evan's voice. "Is Lily's date here?"

His gaze slid past her to the lingerie draped over the foot of her bed. He stared at it for a long moment before shifting his attention back to her.

"I've wanted to talk to you about something."

Her pulse jerked. He was so solemn. This couldn't be good. "You have? Let's go have dinner and chat."

He put up his hands as she started for the door. "This is something we need to discuss, just us."

Nothing that serious could ever be good. "You know, I'm in a really good place right now." She pulled her hair over one shoulder and finger-combed it into three sections. "The practice is booming. Terry wants me to buy him out." Her fingers made quick work of a braid and she snagged a scrunchy off her nightstand. "I'm happy."

"And I don't want that to change. But there's something you need to know—"

"Dinner's ready."

Ming cast her sister a grateful smile. "Wonderful. Come on, Evan. You're in for a treat." She practically raced down the stairs. Her glass of wine was on the counter where she'd left it and Ming downed the contents in one long swallow. Wincing at the taste, she reached into her wine cooler and pulled out a Shiraz.

Over dinner, Evan's sober expression and Lily's preoccupation with her own thoughts compelled Ming to fill the awkward silence with a series of stories about her trip to San Francisco and amusing anecdotes about Wendy's six-year-old daughter.

By the time the kitchen was cleaned up and the dishwasher happily humming, she was light-headed from too much wine and drained from carrying the entire conversation.

Making no attempt to hide her yawns, Ming headed upstairs and shut her bedroom door behind her. In the privacy of her large master suite, she stripped off her clothes and stepped into the shower. The warm water pummeled her, releasing some of the tension from her shoulders. Wrapped in a thick terry-cloth robe, she sat cross-legged on her window seat and stared out over her backyard. She had no idea how long her thoughts drifted before a soft knock sounded on her door.

Lily stuck her head in. "You okay?"

"Is Evan gone?"

Lily nodded. "I'm sorry about what I said to you earlier."

"You're not wrong. I am being selfish." Ming patted the seat beside her. "But at the same time you know that once I decide to do something, I give it my all."

Lily hugged Ming before sitting beside her on the window seat. "If anyone is going to be supermom it's you."

"Thanks." Ming swallowed past the tightness in her throat. She hated fighting with Lily. "So, what's up with Evan?"

"What do you mean?"

"When I came in tonight, he looked as grim as I've ever seen him. I figured he was explaining why he showed up out of the blue." Ming knew her sister had always been partial to Jason's older brother. Often in the past six months, Ming thought Lily had been the sister most upset about the broken engagement. "You two became such good friends these last few years. I thought maybe he'd share with you his reason for coming here tonight."

"Do you think Jason told him that you want to have a baby?"

"He wouldn't do that." Ming's skin grew warm as she imagined where she'd be right at this moment if she hadn't run out on Jason. Naked. Wrapped in his arms. Thighs tangled. Too happy to move. "I know this sounds crazy, but what if Evan wants to get back together?"

"Why would you think he'd want to do that?" Lily's voice rose.

"I don't. Not really." Ming shook her head. "It's just that after I told Jason I wanted to get pregnant, he was so insistent that I'm not over Evan."

"Are you?" Her sister leaned forward, eyebrows drawn together. "I mean Evan broke up with you, not the other way around."

Ming toyed with the belt of her robe. The pain of being dumped eased a little more each day, but it wasn't completely gone. "It really doesn't matter how I feel. The reasons we broke up haven't changed."

"What if they did? What if the problems that came between you were gone? Out of the picture?" Lily was oddly intent. "Would you give him another chance?"

Ming tried to picture herself with Evan now that she'd tasted Jason's kisses. She'd settled for one brother instead of fighting for the other. That was a mistake she wouldn't make again. She'd rather be happy as a single mom than be miserable married to a man she didn't love.

"I've spent the last six months reimagining my life without Evan," she told her sister. "I'd rather move forward than look back."

At a little after 8:00 p.m., Jason sat in his car and stared at Ming's house. When she'd left him in Mendocino, his pride had kept him from chasing after her for a little over two hours. He'd come to California to spend the weekend with Ming, not to pace a hotel room in a frenzy of unsatisfied desire. Confident she wouldn't miraculously change her mind and return to him, Jason had gotten behind the wheel and returned to the San Francisco airport, where he'd caught a 6:00 a.m. flight back to Houston.

He hadn't liked the way things had been left between them, and her text message gave him hope she hadn't, either. After catching a few hours of sleep, he'd come here tonight to talk her into giving his strategy one last shot.

But the sight of his brother's car parked in Ming's driveway distracted him. What the hell was Evan doing here? Had he come to tell Ming that he was dating her sister? If so, Jason should get in there because Ming was sure to be upset.

He had his hand on the door release when her front door opened. Despite the porch light pouring over the couple's head, he couldn't see Lily's expression, but her body language would be visible from the moon.

Ming's sister was hung up on his brother. And from the way Evan slid his hands around her waist and pulled her against him for a deep, passionate kiss, the feeling was mutual.

It took no more than a couple of seconds for an acid to eat at Jason's gut. He glanced away from the embracing couple, but anger continued to build.

What the hell did Evan think he was doing? Didn't he care about Ming's feelings at all? Didn't he consider how hurt she'd be if she saw him kissing Lily? Obviously not. Good thing Jason was around to straighten out his brother before the situation spun out of control.

A motor started, drowning out Jason's heated thoughts. Evan backed out of the driveway. Jason had missed the chance to catch his brother in the act. Cursing, he dialed Evan's number.

"Jason, hey, what's up?"

"We need to talk."

"So talk." Considering the fact that Evan had just engaged in a long, passionate kiss, he wasn't sounding particularly chipper.

"In person." So he could throttle his brother if the urge arose. "O'Malley's. Ten minutes."

The tension in Jason's tone must have clued in his brother to Jason's determination because Evan agreed without protest. "Sure. Okay."

Jason ended the call and followed his brother's car to the neighborhood bar. He chose the parking spot next to Evan's and was standing at his brother's door before Evan had even turned off the engine.

"You and Lily are still seeing each other?" Jason demanded, not allowing his brother to slide from behind the wheel.

"I never said I was going to stop."

"Does Ming know?"

"Not yet."

"She'll find out pretty quickly if you keep kissing Lily in full view of Ming's neighbors."

"I didn't think about that." Evan didn't ask how Jason knew. "I was sure Ming wouldn't see us. She'd gone up to her room."

"So that made it okay?" Fingers curling into fists, Jason stabbed his brother with a fierce glare. "If you intend to flaunt your relationship, you need to tell her what you and Lily are doing."

"I started to tonight, but Lily interrupted me. She doesn't want Ming to know." And Evan didn't look happy about it. "Can we go inside and discuss this over a beer?"

Considering his mood, Jason wasn't sure consuming alcohol around his brother was a wise idea, but he stepped back so Evan could get out of the car. With an effort Jason unclenched his fists and concentrated on soothing his bad temper. By the time they were seated near the back, Jason's fury had become a slow burn.

"Why doesn't Lily want Ming to know?" Jason sat with his spine pressed against the booth's polished wood back while Evan leaned his forearms on the table, all earnest and contrite.

"Because I don't think she intends for it to go anywhere."

If Evan wasn't running the risk of hurting Ming all over again, Jason could have sympathized with his brother's pain. "Then you need to quit seeing her."

"I can't." Despite the throb in his brother's voice, the corners of his mouth relaxed. "The sex is incredible. I tell myself a hundred times a day that it's going nowhere and that I should get out before anyone is hurt, but then I hear her voice or see her and I have to…" He grimaced. "I don't know why I'm telling you this."

"So you two are combustible together." Resentment made Jason cross. He and Ming had great chemistry, too, but instead of exploring some potentially explosive lovemaking, they were at odds over what effect this might have on their friendship.

"It's amazing."

"But…?" Jason prompted.

"I don't know if we can make it work. We have completely different ideas about what we want." Evan shook his head. "And now she's moving to Portland."

Which should put an end to things, but Jason sensed the upcoming separation was causing things to heat up rather than cool down.

"Long-range relationships don't work," Jason said.

"Sometimes they do. And I love her." Something Evan looked damned miserable about.

"Is she in love with you?"

"She claims it's nothing but casual sex between us. But it sure as hell doesn't feel casual when we're at it."

Love was demonstrating once again that it had no one's best interests at heart. Evan was in love with Lily, but she obviously didn't feel the same way, and that made him unhappy. And finding out that her ex-fiancé was in love with her sister was going to cause Ming pain. Nothing good came of falling in love.

"All the more reason you should quit seeing Lily before Ming finds out."

"That's not what I want."

"What *you* want?"

Jason contemplated the passion that tormented his brother. The entire time Evan and Ming were dating, not once had Evan displayed the despair that afflicted him now.

"How about what's good for Ming?" Jason continued.

"Don't you think you did enough damage to her when you broke off your engagement two weeks before the wedding?"

"Yeah, well, that was bad timing on my part." Evan paused for a beat. "We weren't meant to be together."

"You and Lily aren't meant to be together, either."

"I don't agree." Evan sounded grim. "And I want a chance to prove it. Can I count on you to keep quiet?"

"No." Seeing his brother's expression, Jason relented. "I'm not going to run over there tonight and tell her. Talk to Lily. Figure this out. You can have until noon tomorrow."

As his anger over Evan's choice of romantic partner faded, Jason noticed the hollow feeling in his chest was back. He sipped the beer the waitress had set before him and wondered why Ming had chosen to pick a fight with him in California instead of surrendering to the heat between them.

Was she really afraid their relationship would be changed by sex? How could it when they'd been best friends for over twenty years? Sure, there'd been sparks the night of senior prom, but they'd discussed the situation and decided their friendship was more important than trying to date only to have it end badly.

And what they were about to do wasn't dating. It was sex, pure and simple. A way for Ming to get pregnant. For Jason to purge her from his system.

For him to satisfy his curiosity?

Maybe her accusation hadn't been completely off the mark. He wouldn't be a guy if he hadn't looked at Ming in a bathing suit and recognized she was breathtaking. From prom night his fingers knew the shape of her breasts, his tongue the texture of her nipples. The soft heat of her mouth against his. That wasn't something he could experience and then never think about again.

But he wasn't in love with her. He'd never let that happen. Their friendship was too important to mess up with romance. Love had almost killed his father. And Evan wasn't doing too well, either.

Nope. Better to keep things casual. Uncomplicated.

Which didn't explain why he'd offered to help Ming get pregnant and why he'd suggested they do it the natural way. And Jason had no easy answer.

Six

By Sunday afternoon Ming still hadn't heard from Jason, and his lack of response to her phone calls and texts struck her as odd. She'd apologized a dozen times. Why was he avoiding her? After brunch with Lily, she drove to Jason's house in the hope of cornering him and getting answers. Relief swept her as she spied him by the 'Cuda he'd won off Max a few months ago. She parked her car at the bottom of the driveway and stared at him for a long moment.

Bare except for a pair of cargo shorts that rode low on his hips, he was preoccupied with eliminating every bit of dust from the car's yellow paint. His bronzed skin glistened with a fine mist of water from the hole in the nearby garden hose. The muscles across his back rippled as he plunged the sponge into the bucket of soapy water near his bare feet.

Ming imagined gliding her hands over those male contours, digging her nails into his flesh as he devoured her. The fantasy inspired a series of hot flashes. She slid from behind the wheel and headed toward him.

"I think you missed a spot," she called, stopping a couple feet away from the back bumper. Hearing the odd note in her own voice brought about by her earlier musing, she winced. When he frowned at her, she pointed to a nonexistent smudge on the car's trunk.

Since waking at six that morning, she'd been debating what tack to take with Jason. Did she scold him for not calling her back? Did she pretend that she wasn't hurt and worried that he'd ignored her apologies? Or did she just leave her emotional baggage at the door and talk to him straight like a friend?

Jason dropped the sponge on the car's roof and set his hands on his hips. "I'm pretty sure I didn't."

She eyed the car. "I'm pretty sure you did." When he didn't respond, she stepped closer to the car and pointed. "Right here."

"If you think you can do better…" He lobbed the dripping sponge onto the trunk. It landed with a splat, showering her with soapy water. "Go ahead."

Unsure why he got to act unfriendly when she'd been the one to apologize only to be ignored, she picked up the sponge and debated what to do with it. She could toss it back and hope it hit him full in the face, or she could take the high road and see if they could talk through what had happened in California.

Gathering a calming breath, she swept the sponge over the trunk and down toward the taillights. "I've left you a few messages," she said, focusing on the task at hand.

"I know. Sorry I haven't called you back."

"Is there a reason why you didn't?"

"I've been busy."

Cleaning an already pristine car was a pointless endeavor. So was using indirect methods to get Jason to talk about something uncomfortable. "When you didn't call me back, I started wondering if you were mad at me."

"Why would I be mad?"

Ming circled the car and dunked the sponge into the bucket. Jason had retreated to the opposite side of the 'Cuda and was spraying the car with water. Fine mist filled the air, landing on Ming's skin, lightly coating her white blouse and short black skirt. She hadn't come dressed to wash a car. And if she didn't retreat, she risked ruining her new black sandals.

"Because of what happened in Mendocino."

"You mean because you freaked out?" At last he met her gaze. Irritation glittered in his bright blue eyes.

"I didn't freak…exactly."

"You agreed we'd spend three days together and when you got there, you lasted barely an hour before picking a fight with me and running out. How is that not freaking?"

Ming scrubbed at the side mirror, paying careful attention to the task. "Well, I wouldn't have done that if you hadn't gone all Don Juan on me."

"Don Juan?" He sounded incredulous.

"Master of seduction."

"I have no idea what you're talking about."

"The roses on the bed. The vanilla candles. I'm surprised you didn't draw me a bubble bath." In the silence that followed her accusation, she glanced up. The expression on his face told her that had also been on his agenda. "Good grief."

"Forgive me for trying to create a romantic mood."

"I didn't ask for romance," she protested. "I just wanted to get pregnant."

In a clinic. Simple. Uncomplicated.

"Since when do you have something against romance? I seem to remember you liked it when Evan sent you flowers and took you out for candlelit dinners."

"Evan and I were dating." They'd been falling in love.

She picked up the bucket and moved to the front of the car. This time Jason stayed put.

"I thought you'd appreciate the flowers and the candlelight."

Ming snorted. "Men do stuff like that to get women into bed. But you already knew we were going to have sex. So what was with the whole seduction scene?"

"Why are you making such an issue out of this?"

She stopped scrubbing the hood and stared at him, hoping she could make him understand without divulging too much. "You created the perfect setting to make me fall in love with you."

"That's not what I was doing."

"I know you don't plan to make women fall for you, but it's what happens to everyone you date." She applied the sponge to the hood in a fury. "You overwhelm them with romantic gestures until they start picturing a future with you and then you drop them because they want more than you can give them."

The only movement in his face was the tic in his jaw. "You make it sound like I deliberately try to hurt them."

"That's not it at all. I don't think you have any idea what it's like when you turn on the Sterling charm."

"Are you saying that's what I did to you?"

It was the deliberate nature of what he'd done that made her feel like a prize to be won, not a friend to be helped. Another conquest. Another woman who would fall in love with him and then be dumped when she got too serious. When she wanted too much from him.

"Yes. And I don't get why." She dropped the sponge into the bucket and raked her fingers through her damp hair, lifting the soggy weight off her neck and back so the breeze could cool her. "All I wanted was to have a baby. I didn't want to complicate our friendship with sex. Or make things weird between us." Dense emotions weighed on her. Her shoulders sagged beneath the burden. She let her arms fall to her sides. "That's why I've decided to let you off the hook."

"What do you mean?"

"I'm going forward as originally planned. I'll use an anonymous donor and we can pretend the last two weeks never happened."

"I'm tired of pretending."

Before she'd fully processed his statement, chilly water rained down on her. Ming shrieked and stepped back.

"Hey." She wiped water from her eyes and glared at Jason. "Watch it."

"Sorry." But he obviously wasn't.

"You did that on purpose."

"I didn't."

"Did, too."

And abruptly they were eight again, chasing each other around her parents' backyard with squirt guns. She grabbed the sponge out of the bucket and tossed it at his head. He dodged it without even moving his feet, and a smattering of droplets showered down on her.

The bucket of water was at her feet. Seconds later it was in her hands. She didn't stop to consider the consequences of what she was about to do. How long since she'd acted without thought?

"If you throw that, I'll make sure you'll regret it," Jason warned, his serious tone a stark contrast to the dare in his eyes.

The emotional tug-of-war of the past two weeks had taken a toll on her. Her friendship with Jason was the foundation that she'd built her life on. But the longing for his kisses, the anticipation of his hands sliding over her naked flesh… She was on fire for him. Head and heart at war.

"Damn you, Jason," she whispered.

Soapy water arced across the six feet separating them and landed precisely where she meant it to. Drenched from head to groin, Jason stood perfectly still for as long as it took for Ming to drop the bucket. Then he gave his head a vigorous shake, showering soapy droplets all around him.

Ming watched as if in slow motion as he raised the hose in his hand, aimed it at her and squeezed the trigger. Icy water sprayed her. Sputtering with laughter, she put up her hands and backed away. Hampered by her heels from moving fast enough to escape, she shrieked for Jason to stop. When the deluge continued, she kicked off her shoes and raced for the house.

Until she stood dripping on Jason's kitchen floor, it hadn't occurred to her why she hadn't made a break for her car. The door leading to the garage slammed shut.

Shivering in the air-conditioning, Ming whirled to confront Jason.

He stalked toward her. Eyes on fire. Mouth set in a grim line. She held her ground as he drew near. Her trembling became less about being chilled and more about Jason's intensity as he stepped into her space and cupped her face in his hands.

"I'm sorry about California…"

The rest of her words were lost, stopped by the demanding press of his lips to hers. Electrified by the passion in his kiss, she rose up on tiptoe and wrapped her arms around his neck and let him devour her with lips, tongue and teeth.

Yes. This is what she'd been waiting for. The crazy wildness that had gripped them on prom night. The urgent craving to rip each other's clothes off and couple like long-lost lovers. Fire exploded in her loins as pulse after pulse drove heat to her core.

She drank from the passion in his kiss, found her joy in the feint and retreat of his tongue with hers. His hands left her face and traveled down her throat to her shoulders. And lower. She quaked as his palms moved over her breasts and caressed her stomach. Before she knew what he was after, he'd gathered handfuls of her blouse. She felt a tremor ripple through his torso a second before he tore her shirt open.

Flinging off her ruined shirt, Ming arched her back and pressed into his palms as he cupped her breasts through her sodden bra and made her nipples peak. Between her thighs an ache built toward a climax that would drive her mad if she couldn't get him to hurry. Impatience clawed at her. She needed his skin against hers. Reaching behind her, Ming released her bra clasp.

Jason peeled it away and drew his fingertips around her

breasts and across her aching nipples. "Perfect." Husky with awe, his voice rasped against her nerves, inflaming her already raging desire.

He bent his head and took one pebbled bud into his mouth, rolling his tongue over the hard point before sucking hard. The wet pulling sensation shot a bolt of sensation straight to where she hungered, wrenching a gasp from Ming.

"Do that again," she demanded, her fingers biting into his biceps. "That was incredible."

He obliged until her knees threatened to give out. "I've imagined you like this for so long," he muttered against her throat, teeth grazing the cord in her neck.

"Like what, half-naked?"

"Trembling. On fire." He slipped his hand beneath her skirt and skimmed up her thigh. "For me."

Shuddering as he closed in on the area where she wanted him most, Ming let her own fingers do some exploring. Behind the zipper of his cargo shorts he was huge and hard. As her nails grazed along his length, Jason closed his eyes. Breath escaped in a hiss from between his clenched teeth.

Happy with his reaction, but wanting him as needy as he'd made her, she unfastened his shorts and dived beneath the fabric to locate skin. A curse escaped him when she sent his clothes to pool at his feet. She grasped him firmly.

Abandoning his own exploration, he pulled her hands away and carried them around to his back. His mouth settled on hers again, this time stealing her breath and her sense of equilibrium. She was spinning. Twirling. Lost in the universe. Only Jason's mouth on hers, his arms banding her body to his, gave her any sense of reality.

This is what she'd been missing on the couch in his den and on the deck in California. The line between friend and lover wasn't just blurred, it was eradicated by hunger and wanton impulses. Hesitations were put aside. There was only heat and urgency. Demand and surrender.

Her back bumped against something. She opened her eyes as Jason's lips left hers.

"I need you now," she murmured as he nibbled down her neck.

"Let's go upstairs."

Her knees wouldn't survive the climb. "I can't make it that far."

"What do you have in mind?"

His kitchen table caught her eye. "How about this?"

Her knees had enough strength to back him up five feet. He looked surprised when she shoved him onto one of the four straight-back chairs.

"I'm game if you are."

She hadn't finished shimmying out of her skirt when she felt his fingers hook in the waistband of her hot pink thong and begin drawing it down her thighs. Naked, she stared down at him, her heart pinging around in her chest.

There was no turning back from this moment.

Jason's fingers bit into her hips as she straddled the chair. Meeting his gaze, she positioned herself so the tip of him grazed her entrance. Looking into his eyes, she could see straight to his soul. No veils hid his emotions from her.

She lowered herself, joining them in body as in spirit, let her head fall back and gloried at the perfection of their fit.

He'd died and gone to heaven. With Ming arched over his arm, almost limp in his grasp, he'd reached a nirvana of sorts. The sensation of being buried inside her almost blew the top of his head off. He shuddered, lost in a bewildering maze of emotions.

"This is the first time," he muttered, lowering his lips to her throat, "I've never done this before."

She tightened her inner muscles around him and he groaned. Her chest vibrated in what sounded like a laugh. With her fingers digging into his shoulders, she straightened and stared deep into his eyes.

"I have it on good authority," she began, leaning forward to draw her tongue along his lower lip, "that this is not your first time." She spoke without rancor, unbothered by the women he'd been with before.

He stroked his hands up her spine, fingers gliding over her silken skin, feeling the ridges made by her ribs. "It's the first I've ever had sex without protection."

"Really?" She peered at him from beneath her lashes. "I'm your first?"

"My only."

The instant the words were out, Jason knew he'd said too much. Delight flickered in her gaze. Her glee lasted only for the briefest of instances, but he'd spotted it, knew what he'd given away.

"I like the sound of that."

"Only because I am never going to get anyone but you pregnant."

Her smile transformed her from serene and mysterious to animated and exotic. "I like the sound of that, too." This time when she kissed him, there was no teasing in her actions. She took his mouth, plunged her tongue deep and claimed him.

Fisting a hand in her hair, Jason answered her primal call. Their tongues danced in familiar rhythm, as if they hadn't had their first kiss over a decade before. He knew exactly how to drive her wild, what made her groan and tremble.

"I'll let you in on a little secret," she whispered, her breath hot in his ear. "You're my first, too."

Incapable of speech as she explored his chest, her clever fingers circling his nipples, nails raking across their sensitive surface, he arched his brow at her in question.

"I've never had sex on a kitchen chair before." She rotated her hips in a sexy figure eight that wrenched a groan from his throat. "I rather like it."

Pressure built in his groin as she continued to experiment with her movements. Straddling his lap, she had all the control she could ever want to drive him mad. Breath rasping, eyes half-closed, Jason focused on her face to distract himself from the pleasure cascading through his body. In all the dreams he'd had of her, nothing had been this perfect.

Arching her back, she shifted the angle of her hips and moved over him again. "Oh, Jason, this is incredible."

"Amazing." He garbled the word, provoking a short laugh from her. "Perfect."

"Yes." She sat up straight and looked him square in the eyes. "It's never been like this."

"For me, either."

Deciding they'd done enough talking, Jason kissed her, long and deep. Her movements became more urgent as their passion burned hotter. His fingers bit into her hips, guiding her. A soft cry slipped from her parted lips. Jason felt her body tense and knew she was close. That's all it took to start his own climax. Gaze locked on her face, he held back, waiting for her to pitch over the cliff. The sheer glory of it caught him off guard. She gave herself completely to the moment. And called his name.

With his ears filled with her rapture, he lost control and spilled himself inside her. They were making more than a baby. They were making a moment that would last forever. The richness of the experience shocked him. Never in a million years would he have guessed that letting himself go so completely would hit him with this sort of power.

Shaking, Jason gathered Ming's body tight against his chest and breathed heavily. As the last pulses of her orgasm eased, he smoothed her hair away from her face and bestowed a gentle kiss on her lips.

"I'm glad I was your first," she murmured, her slender arms wrapped around his neck.

He smiled. "I'm glad you're my only."

* * *

Taking full advantage of Jason's king-size bed, Ming lay on her stomach lengthwise across the mattress. With her chin on his chest, her feet kicking the air, she watched him. Naked and relaxed, he'd stretched out on his back, his hands behind his head, eyes closed, legs crossed at the ankle. An easy smile tipped the corners of his lips upward. Ming regarded his satisfied expression, delighted that she'd been the one to bring him to this state. Twice.

While her body was utterly drained of energy, the same couldn't be said for her mind. "Now that we have that out of the way, perhaps you can explain why you've been avoiding me for two days."

Jason's expression tightened. "Have you talked to your sister?"

"Lily?" Ming pushed herself into a sitting position. "We had brunch before I came here. Why?"

His lashes lifted. "She didn't tell you."

She had no idea what he was talking about. "Tell me what?"

"About her and Evan." Jason looked unhappy. "They've been seeing each other."

"My sister and your brother?" Ming repeated the words but couldn't quite get her mind around the concept. "Seeing other…you mean dating?"

Her gaze slid over Jason. Two weeks ago she'd have laughed at anyone who told her she and Jason were going to end up in bed together. The news of Evan and Lily was no less unexpected.

"Yes." He touched her arm, fingers gentle as they stroked her skin. "Are you okay?"

His question startled her. But it was the concern on his face that made her take stock of her reaction. To her dismay she felt a twinge of discomfort. But she'd be damned if she'd admit it.

"If they get married we'll end up being brother and sister." She was trying for levity but fell short of the mark.

Jason huffed out an impatient breath. "Don't make light of this with me. I'm worried that you'll end up getting hurt."

Ming's bravado faded. "But it can't be that serious. Lily is moving to Portland. She wouldn't be doing that if they had a future together." Her voice trailed away. "That's why she's leaving, isn't it? They're in love and my sister can't break it off and stick around. She needs to move thousands of miles away to get over him."

"I don't know if your sister is in love with Evan."

"But Evan's in love with her."

Jason clamped his mouth shut, but the truth was written all over his face.

Needing a second to recover her equilibrium, Ming left the bed and snagged Jason's robe off the bathroom door. She put it on and fastened the belt around her waist. By the time she finished rolling up the sleeves, she felt calmer and more capable of facing Jason.

"How long have you known?" Ming heard the bitterness in her voice and tried to reel in her emotions. Evan hadn't exactly broken her heart when he'd ended their engagement, but that didn't mean she hadn't been hurt. She'd been weeks away from committing to him for the rest of her life.

"I've known they were going out but didn't realize how serious things had gotten until I spoke with Evan last night." Jason left the bed and came toward her. "Are you okay?"

"Sure." Something tickled her cheek. Ming reached up to touch the spot and her fingers came away wet. "I'm fine."

"Then why are you crying?"

Her heart pumped sluggishly. "I'm feeling sorry for myself because I'm wondering if Evan ever loved me." She stared at the ceiling, blinking hard to hold back the tears. "Am I so unlovable?"

Jason's arms came around her. His lips brushed her cheek. "You're the furthest thing from unlovable."

Safe in his embrace, she badly wanted to believe him, but

the facts spoke loud and clear. She was thirty-one, had never been married and was contemplating single motherhood.

"One of these days you'll find the right guy for you. I'm sure of it."

Hearing Jason's words was like stepping on broken glass. Pain shot through her, but she had nowhere to run. The man her heart had chosen had no thought of ever falling in love with her.

Ming pushed out of Jason's arms. "Did you really just say that minutes after we finished making love?"

His expression darkened. "I'm trying to be a good friend."

"I get that we're never going to be a couple, but did it ever occur to you that I might not be thinking about another man while being naked with you?" Her breath rushed past the lump in her throat.

"That's funny." His voice cracked like a whip. "Because just a second ago you were crying over the fact that my brother is in love with your sister."

Ming's mouth popped open, but no words emerged. Too many statements clogged the pathway between her brain and her lips. Everything Jason had said to her was perfectly reasonable. Her reactions were not. She was treating him like a lover, not like a friend.

"You're right. I'm a little thrown by what's happening between Lily and Evan. But it's not because I'm in love with him. And I can't even think about meeting someone and starting a relationship right now."

"Don't shut yourself off to the possibility."

"Like you have?" Ming couldn't believe he of all people was giving her advice on her love life. Before she blurted out her true feelings, she gathered up all her wayward emotions and packed them away. "I'd better get home and check on Muffin."

"I'm sure Muffin is fine." Jason peered at her, his impatience banked. "Are you?"

"I'm fine."

"Why don't I believe you?"

She wanted to bask in his concern, but they were in different places in their relationship right now. His feelings for her hadn't changed while she was dangerously close to being in love with him.

"No need to worry about me." Ming collected her strength and gave him her best smile. Crossing to his dresser, she pulled out a T-shirt. "Is it okay if I borrow this since you ruined my blouse?"

Jason eyed her, obviously not convinced by her performance. "Go ahead. I don't want to be responsible for any multicar pile-ups if you drive home topless." His tone was good-natured, but his eyes followed her somberly as she exchanged shirt for robe and headed toward the door.

"I'll call you later," she tossed over her shoulder, hoping to escape before unhappiness overwhelmed her.

"You could stay for dinner." He'd accompanied her downstairs and scooped up her black skirt and her hot pink thong before she could reach them, holding them hostage while he awaited her answer.

"I have some case files to look over before tomorrow," she said, conscious of his gaze on her as she tugged her underwear and skirt from his hands.

"You can work on them after dinner. I have some reports to go over. We can have a study date just like old times."

As tempting as that sounded, she recognized that it was time to be blunt. "I need some time to think."

"About what?"

"Things," she murmured, knowing Jason would never let her get away with such a vague excuse. Like how she needed to adjust to being friends *and* lovers with Jason. Then there was the tricky situation with her sister. She needed to get past being angry with Lily, not because she was dating Ming's ex-fiancé, but because her sister might get what Ming couldn't: a happily-ever-after with a man who loved her.

"What is there to think about?" Jason demanded. "We made love. Hopefully, we made a baby."

Her knees knocked together. Could she be pregnant already? The idea thrilled her. She wanted to be carrying Jason's child. Wanted it now more than ever. Which made her question her longing to become a mother. Would she be as determined if it was any other man who was helping her get pregnant? Or was she motivated by the desire to have something of Jason otherwise denied to her?

"I hope that, too." She forced a bright smile.

His bare feet moved soundlessly on the tile floor as he picked up her ruined blouse and carried it to the trash. Slipping back into her clothes, she regarded him in helpless fascination.

In jeans and a black T-shirt, he was everything she'd ever wanted in a man, flaws and all. Strong all the time, sensitive when he needed to be. He demonstrated a capacity for tenderness when she least expected it. They were incredible together in bed and the best of friends out of it.

"Or are you heading home to fret about your sister and Evan seeing each other?"

"No." But she couldn't make her voice as convincing as she wanted it to sound. "Evan and I are over. It was inevitable that he would start dating someone."

She just wished it hadn't happened with her sister.

Ming lifted on her tiptoes and kissed Jason. "Thanks for a lovely afternoon." The spontaneous encounter had knocked her off plan. She needed to regroup and reassess. Aiming for casual, she teased, "Let me know if you feel like doing it again soon."

He grabbed her hand and pushed it against his zipper. "I feel like doing it again now." His husky voice and the intense light in his eyes made her pulse rocket. "Stay for dinner. I promise you won't leave hungry."

The heat of him melted some of the chill from her heart. She leaned into his chest, her fingers curving around the bulge in his pants. He fisted his hand in her hair while his mouth slanted over hers, spiriting her into a passionate whirlwind. This afternoon she'd awakened to his hunger. The power of it set her senses ablaze. She was helpless against the appeal of his hard body as he eased her back against the counter. On the verge of surrendering to the mind-blasting pleasure of Jason's fingers sliding up her naked thigh, his earlier words came back to her.

One of these days you'll find the right guy for you.

She broke off the kiss. Gasping air into her lungs, she put her hands on Jason's chest and ducked her head before he could claim her lips again.

"I've really got to go," she told him, applying enough pressure to assure him she wasn't going to be swayed by his sensual persuasion.

His hands fell away. As hot as he'd been a moment ago, when he stepped back and plunged his hands into his pockets, his blue eyes were as cool and reflective as a mountain lake.

"How about we have dinner tomorrow?" she cajoled, swamped by anxiety. As perfect as it was to feel his arms tighten around her, she needed to sort out her chaotic emotions before she saw him again.

"Sure." Short and terse.

"Here?"

"If you want." He gave her a stiff nod.

She put her hand on his cheek, offered him a glimpse of her longing. "I want very much."

His eyes softened. "Five o'clock." He pressed a kiss into her palm. "Don't be late."

Seven

Ming parked her car near the bleachers that overlooked the curvy two-mile track. Like most of the raceways where Jason spent his weekends, this one was in the middle of nowhere. At least it was only a couple of hours out of Houston. Some of the tracks he raced at were hundreds of miles away.

Jason was going to be surprised to see her. It had been six or seven years since she'd last seen him race. The sport didn't appeal to her. Noisy. Dusty. Monotonous. She suspected the thrills came from driving, not watching.

So, what was she doing here?

If she was acting like Jason's "friend," she would have remained in Houston and spent her Saturday shopping or boating with college classmates. Driving over a hundred miles to sit on a metal seat in the blazing-hot sun fell put her smack dab in the middle of "girlfriend" territory. Would Jason see it as such? Ming took a seat in the stands despite the suspicion that coming here had been a colossal mistake.

The portion of track in front of her was a half-mile drag

strip that allowed the cars to reach over a hundred miles an hour before they had to power down to make the almost ninety-degree turn at the end. The roar was impressive as twenty-five high-performance engines raced past Ming.

Despite the speed at which they traveled, Jason's Mustang was easy to spot. Galaxy-blue. When he'd been working on the car, he'd asked for her opinion and she'd chosen the color, amused that she'd matched his car to his eyes without him catching on.

In seconds, the cars roared off, leaving Ming baking in the hot sun. With her backside sore from the hard bench and her emotions a jumble, it was official. She was definitely exhibiting "girlfriend" behavior.

And why? Because the past week with Jason had been amazing. It wasn't just the sex. It was the intimacy. They'd talked for hours. Laughed. She'd discovered a whole new Jason. Tender and romantic. Naughty and creative. She'd trusted him to take her places she'd never been, and it was addictive.

Which is why she'd packed a bag and decided to surprise him. A single day without Jason had made her restless and unable to concentrate.

Ming stood. This had been a mistake. She wasn't Jason's girlfriend. She had no business inserting herself into his guy time because she was feeling lonely and out of sorts. She would just drive back to Houston and he'd never know how close she'd come to making a complete fool of herself over him.

The cars roared up the straightaway toward her once again. From past experience at these sorts of events, she knew the mornings were devoted to warm-up laps. The real races would begin in the afternoon.

She glanced at the cars as they approached. Jason's number twenty-two was in the middle of the pack of twenty-five cars. He usually saved his best driving for the race. As the Mustang reached the end of the straightaway and began to slow down for the sharp turn, something happened. Instead of curving to the left, the Mustang veered to the right, hit the wall and spun.

Her lungs were ready to burst as she willed the cars racing behind him to steer around the wreckage so Jason didn't suffer any additional impact. Once the track cleared, his pit crew and a dozen others hurried to the car. Dread encased Ming's feet in concrete as she plunged down the stairs to the eight-foot-high chain-link fence that barred her from the track.

With no way of getting to Jason, she was forced to stand by and wait for some sign that he was okay. She gripped the metal, barely registering the ache in her fingers. The front of the Mustang was a crumpled mess. Ming tried to remind herself that the car had been constructed to keep the driver safe during these sorts of crashes, but her emotions, already in a state of chaos before the crash, convinced her he would never hear how she really felt about him.

"Wow, that was some crash," said a male voice beside her. "Worst I've seen in a year."

Ming turned all her fear and angst on the skinny kid with the baseball cap who'd come up next to her. "Do you work here?"

"Ah, yeah." His eyes widened as the full brunt of her emotions hit him.

"I need to get down there, right now."

"You're really not supposed—"

"Right now!"

"Sure. Sure." He backed up a step. "Follow me." He led her to a gate that opened onto the track. "Be careful."

But she was already on the track, pelting toward Jason's ruined car without any thought to her own safety. Because of the dozen or so men gathered around the car, she couldn't see Jason. Wielding her elbows and voice like blunt instruments, she worked her way to the front of the crowd in time to see Jason pulled through the car's window.

He was cursing as he emerged, but he was alive. Relief slammed into her. She stopped five feet from the car and watched him shake off the hands that reached for him when he swayed. He limped toward the crumpled hood, favoring his left knee.

Jason pulled off his helmet. "Damn it, there's the end of my season."

It could have been the end of him. Ming sucked in a breath as a sharp pain lanced through her chest. It was just typical of him to worry about his race car instead of himself. Didn't he realize what losing him would do to the people who loved him?

She stepped up and grabbed his helmet from his hands, but she lost the ability to speak as his eyes swung her way. She loved him. And not like a friend. As a man she wanted to claim for her own.

"Ming?" Dazed, he stared at her as if she'd appeared in a puff of smoke. "What are you doing here?"

"I came to watch you race." She gripped his helmet hard enough to crack it. "I saw you crash. Are you okay?"

"My shoulder's sore and I think I did something to my knee, but other than that, I'm great." His lips twisted as he grimaced. "My car's another thing entirely."

Who cares about your stupid car? Shock made her want to shout at him, but her chest was so tight she had only enough air for a whisper. "You really scared me."

"Jason, we need to get the car off the track." Gus Stover and his brother had been part of Jason's racing team for the past ten years. They'd modified and repaired all his race cars. Ming had lost track of how many hours she and Jason had spent at the man's shop.

"That's a good idea," she said.

"A little help?" Jason suggested after his first attempt at putting weight on his injured knee didn't go so well.

Ming slipped her arm around his waist and began moving in the direction of the pit area. As his body heat began to warm her, Ming realized she was shaking from reaction. As soon as they reached a safe distance from the track, Jason stopped walking and turned her to face him.

"You're trembling. Are you okay?"

Not even close. She loved him. And had for a long time. Only she'd been too scared to admit it to herself.

"I should be asking you that question," she said, placing her palm against his unshaven cheek, savoring the rasp of his beard against her skin. She wanted to wrap her arms around him and never let go. "You should get checked out."

"I'm just a little banged up, that's all."

"Jason, that was a bad crash." A man in his late-thirties with prematurely graying hair approached as they neared the area where the trailers were parked. He wore a maroon racing suit and carried his helmet under one arm. "You okay?"

"Any crash you can walk away from is a good one." Leave it to Jason to make light of something as disastrous as what she'd just witnessed. "Ming, this is Jim Pearce. He's the current points leader in the Texas region."

"And likely to remain on top now that Jason's done for the season."

Is that all these men thought about? Ming's temper began to simmer again until she saw the worry the other driver was masking with his big, confident grin and his posturing. It could have been any of these guys. Accidents didn't happen a lot, but they were part of racing. This was only Jason's second in the entire sixteen years he'd been racing. If something had gone wrong on another area of the track, he might have ended up driving safely onto the shoulder or he could have taken out a half dozen other cars.

"Nice to meet you." As she shook Jim's hand, some of the tension in her muscles eased. "Were you on the track when it happened?"

"No. I'm driving in the second warm-up lap." His broad smile dimmed. "Any idea what happened, Jason? From where I stood it looked like something gave on the right side."

"Felt like the right front strut rod. We recently installed Agent 47 suspension and might have adjusted a little too aggressively on the front-end alignment settings."

Jim nodded, his expression solemn. "Tough break."

"I'll have the rest of the year to get her rebuilt and be back better than ever in January."

Ming contemplated the hours Jason and the Stover brothers would have to put in to make that happen and let her breath out in a long, slow sigh. If she'd seen little of him in the past few months since he'd made it his goal to take the overall points trophy, she'd see even less of him with a car to completely rebuild.

"The Stovers will get her all fixed up for you." Jim thumped Jason on the back. "They're tops."

As Jim spoke, Jason's car was towed up to the trailer. The men in question jumped off the truck and began unfastening the car.

"What happened?" Jason called.

"The strut rod pulled away from the helm end," Gus Stover replied. "I told you the setting was wrong."

His brother, Kris, shook his head. "It's so messed up from the crash, we won't know for sure until we get her on the lift."

"Do you guys need help?" Jason called.

Jim waved and headed off. Ming understood his exit. When Jason and the Stovers started talking cars, no one else on the planet existed. She stared at the ruined car and the group of men who'd gathered to check out the damage. It would be the talk of the track for the rest of the weekend.

"Looks like you've got your hands full," she told Jason, nodding toward a trio of racers approaching them. "I'm going to get out of here so you can focus on the Mustang."

"Wait." He caught her hand, laced his fingers through hers. "Stick around."

She melted beneath the heat of his smile. "I'll just be in the way."

"I need you—"

"Jason, that was some crash," the man in the middle said.

Ming figured she'd take advantage of the interruption to escape, but Jason refused to relinquish her hand. A warm feeling set up shop in her midsection as Jason introduced her. She'd expected once his buddies surrounded him, he wouldn't care if she took off.

But after an hour she lost all willpower to do so. Despite the attention Jason received from his fellow competitors, he never once forgot that she was there. Accustomed to how focused Jason became at the track, Ming was caught off guard by the way he looped his arm around her waist and included her in the conversations.

By the time the car had been packed up later that afternoon, she was congratulating herself on her decision to come. They sat side by side on the tailgate of his truck. Jason balanced an icepack on his injured knee. Despite the heat, she was leaning against his side, enjoying the lean strength of his body.

"What prompted you to come to the track today?" he questioned, gaze fixed on the Stover brothers as they argued over how long it would take them to get the car ready to race once more.

The anxiety that had gripped her before his crash reappeared and she shrugged to ease her sudden tension. "It's been a long time since I've seen you race." She eyed the busted-up Mustang. "And now it's going to be even longer."

"So it seems."

"Sorry your season ended like this. Are you heading back tonight?"

"Gus and Kris are. I've got a hotel room in town. I think I'll ice my knee and drive back tomorrow."

She waited a beat, hoping he'd ask her to stay, but no invitation was forthcoming. "Want company?"

"In the shape I'm in, I'd be no use to you." He shot her a wry smile.

As his friend, she shouldn't feel rejected, but after accepting that she was in love with him and being treated like his girlfriend all day, she'd expected he'd want her to stick around. She recognized that he was in obvious pain and needed a restful night's sleep. A friend would put his welfare above her own desires.

"Then I guess I'll head back to Houston." She kissed him on the cheek and hopped off the tailgate.

He caught her wrist as her feet hit the ground. "I'm really glad you came today."

It wasn't fair the way he turned the sex appeal on and off whenever it suited him. Ming braced herself against the lure of his sincere eyes and enticing smile. Had she fallen in love with his charm? If so, could she go back to being just his friend once they stopped sleeping together?

She hoped so. Otherwise she'd spend the rest of her life in love with a man who would never let himself love her back.

"Supporting each other is what friends are for," she said, stepping between his thighs and taking his face in her hands.

Slowly she brought her lips to his, releasing all her pent-up emotions into the kiss. Her longing for what she could never have. Her fear over his brush with serious injury. And pure, sizzling desire.

After the briefest of hesitations, he matched her passion, fingers digging into her back as he fed off her mouth. The kiss exhilarated her. Everything about being with Jason made her happy. Smiling, she sucked his lower lip into her mouth and rubbed her breasts against his chest. As soon as she heard his soft groan, she released him.

Stepping back, Ming surveyed her handiwork. From the dazed look in his eyes, the flush darkening his cheekbones and the unsteady rush of breath in and out of his lungs, the kiss had packed a wallop. A quick glance below his belt assured her he would spend a significant portion of the evening thinking about her. Good.

"Careful on the drive home tomorrow," she murmured, wiping her fingertip across her damp lips in deliberate seduction. "Call me when you get back."

And with a saucy wave, she headed for her car.

The sixty-eight-foot cruiser Jason had borrowed for Max's bachelor party barely rocked as it encountered the wake of the large powerboat that had sped across their bow seconds earlier. Cigar in one hand, thirty-year-old Scotch in the other, Jason tracked the boat skimming the dark waters of Galveston Bay from upstairs in the open-air lounge. On the opposite rail, Max's brothers were discussing their wives and upcoming fatherhood.

"She's due tomorrow," Nathan Case muttered, tapping his cell phone on his knee. "I told her it was crazy for me come to this bachelor party, but she was determined to go out dancing with Missy, Rachel and her friends."

Nathan's aggrieved tone found a sympathetic audience in Jason. Why were women so calm about the whole pregnancy-and-giving-birth thing? Ming wasn't even pregnant, and Jason was already experiencing a little coil of tension deep in his gut. He hadn't considered how connected he'd feel to her when he'd agreed to father her baby. Nor could he stop wondering if he'd feel as invested if they'd done it her way and he'd never made love to her.

"I'm sure Emma knows what she's doing," Sebastian Case said. Older than Max and Nathan by a few years, Sebastian was every inch the confident CEO of a multimillion-dollar corporation.

"I think she's hoping the dancing will get her contractions started." Nathan stared at the cell phone as if he could make it ring by sheer willpower. "What if her water breaks on the dance floor?"

"Then she'll call and you can meet her at the hospital." Sebastian's soothing tones were having little effect on his agitated half brother.

"You're barely into your second trimester," Nathan scoffed. "Let's see how rational you are when Missy hasn't been able to see her feet for a month, doesn't sleep more than a few hours a night and can't go ten minutes without finding a bathroom."

Sebastian's eyes grew distant for a few seconds as if he was imagining his wife in the final weeks before she was due.

"Do you know what you're having?" Even as Jason asked Nathan the question, he realized that a month ago he never would have thought to inquire.

"A boy."

Jason lifted his Scotch in a salute. "Congratulations."

"You're single, aren't you?" Sebastian regarded him like a curiosity. "How come you're not downstairs with Max and his buddies slipping fives into the ladies' G-strings instead of hanging out with a couple old family men?"

Because he wasn't feeling particularly single at the moment.

Jason raised the cigar. "Charlie said no smoking in the salon."

"But you're missing the entertainment." Nathan gestured toward the stairs that led below.

Some entertainment. Max might be downstairs with a half dozen of their single friends and a couple of exotic dancers someone had hired, but Jason doubted his best friend was having any fun. Max wasn't interested in any woman except Rachel.

Up until two weeks ago Jason hadn't understood what had come over his friend. Now, after making love with Ming, his craving for her had taken on a life of its own. His body stirred at the memory of her dripping wet in his kitchen. The way her white blouse had clung to her breasts, the fabric rendered sheer by the water. He wasn't sure what he would have done if she'd denied him then. Gotten down on his knees and begged?

Probably.

Jason shoved aside the unsettling thought and smirked at Nathan. "When you're free to hit a strip club any night of the week, the novelty wears off. You two are the ones who should be downstairs."

"Why's that?" Nathan asked.

"I just assumed with your wives being pregnant…"

Sebastian and Nathan exchanged amused looks.

"That our sex lives are nonexistent?" Sebastian proposed. He looked as relaxed and contented as a lion after consuming an antelope.

The last emotion pestering Jason should be envy. He was the free one. Unfettered by emotional ties that had the potential to do damage. Unhampered by monotony, he was free to sleep with a different woman every night of the week if he wanted. He had no demanding female complicating his days.

"Did it surprise either of you that Max is getting married?" Jason asked.

Sebastian swirled the Scotch in his glass. "If I had to wager which one of you two would be getting married first, I would have bet on you."

"Me?" Jason shook his head in bafflement.

"I thought for sure you and Ming would end up together."

"We're close friends, nothing more."

Sebastian's thumb traced the rim of his glass. "Yeah, it took me a long time to see what was waiting right under my nose, too."

Rather than sputter out halfhearted denials, Jason downed the last of his drink and stubbed out the cigar. The Scotch scorched a trail from his throat to his chest.

"I think I'll go see if Max needs rescuing."

They'd been cruising around Galveston for a little over an hour and Jason was as itchy to get off the boat as Nathan. He wanted to blame his restlessness on the fact that the bachelor party meant a week from now his relationship with his best buddy would officially go on the back burner as Max took on his new responsibilities as a husband. But Max had been splitting his loyalty for three months now, and Jason was accustomed to being an afterthought.

No, Jason's edginess was due to the fact that like Nathan, Sebastian and Max, he'd rather be with the woman he was intimate with than whooping it up with a bunch of single guys and a couple of strippers.

What had happened to him?

Only two weeks ago he'd been moaning that Max had abandoned him for a woman. And here he was caught in the same gossamer net, pining for a particular female's companionship.

He met Max on the narrow stairs that connected the salon level to the upper deck, where Nathan and Sebastian remained.

"Feel like getting off this boat and hooking up with our ladies?" Max proposed. "I just heard from Rachel. They've had their fill of the club."

Jason glanced at his watch. "It's only ten-thirty. This is your bachelor party. You're supposed to get wild one last time before you're forever leg-shackled to one woman."

"I'd rather get wild with the woman I'm going to be leg-shackled to." Max punched Jason in the shoulder. "Besides, I don't see you downstairs getting a lap dance from either Candy or Angel."

"Charlie said no smoking in the salon. I went upstairs to enjoy one of the excellent cigars Nathan brought."

"And this has nothing to do with the warning you gave Ming tonight?"

Jason cursed. "You heard that?"

"I thought it was cute."

"Jackass." Swearing at Max was a lot easier than asking himself why he'd felt compelled to tell Ming to behave herself and not break any hearts at the club. He'd only been half joking. The thought of her contemplating romance with another man aroused some uncomfortably volatile emotions.

"And it doesn't look like she listened to you."

"What makes you say that?"

Max showed him his cell phone screen. "I think this guy's pretty close to having his heart broken."

Jason swallowed a growl but could do nothing about the frown that pulled his brows together when he glimpsed the photo of Ming dancing with some guy. Irritation fired in his gut. It wasn't the fact that Ming had her head thrown back and her arms above her head that set Jason off. It was the way the guy had his hands inches from her hips and looked prepared to go where no one but Jason belonged.

Max laughed. "I know Nathan and Sebastian are ready to leave. Are you up for taking the launch in and leaving the boys to play by themselves?"

Damn right he was. "This is your party. Where you go, I go."

Eight

Rachel Lansing, bride-to-be, laughed at the photo her fiancé sent her from his bachelor party. Sitting across the limo from her, Ming wasn't the least bit amused. Her stomach had been churning for the last half an hour, ever since she'd found out that there were exotic dancers on the boat. And her anxiety hadn't been relieved when she hadn't spotted Jason amongst the half dozen men egging on the strippers. He could be standing behind Max, out of the camera's range.

She had no business feeling insecure and suspicious. It wasn't as if she had a claim to Jason beyond their oh-so-satisfying baby-making activities. Problem was, she couldn't disconnect her emotions. And heaven knew she'd been trying to. Telling herself over and over that it was just sex. Incredibly hot, passionate, mind-blowing sex, but not the act of two people in love. Just a couple of friends trying to make a baby together.

Whom was she kidding?

For the past two weeks, she'd been deliriously happy and anxiety-ridden by turn. Every time he slid inside her it was a struggle not to confide that she was falling in love with him, and her strength was fading fast. Already she was rationalizing why she and Jason should continue to be intimate long after she was pregnant.

It was only a matter of time before she confessed what she truly wanted for her future and he'd sit her down and remind her why they'd made love in the first place. Then things would get awkward and they'd start to avoid each other. No. Better to stay silent and keep Jason as her best friend rather than lose him forever.

"If you're worried about Jason, Max texted me and said he's on the upper deck with Nathan and Sebastian." Rachel gave Ming a reassuring smile.

"I'm not worried about Jason," Ming hastily assured her as she sagged in relief. She mustered a smile. "No need for me to be. We're just friends. Have been for years."

A fact Rachel knew perfectly well since the four of them had gone out numerous times since she and Max had gotten engaged. Ming had no idea why she had to keep reminding people that she and Jason were not an item.

"Jason's a great guy."

"He sure is." Ming saw where this was going and knew she had to cut Rachel off. "But he's the sort of guy who isn't ever going to fall in love and get married."

Rachel cocked her head. "Funny, that's what I thought about Max and yet he lost his favorite car to Jason over a wager that he wouldn't get married." Her blue eyes sparkled with mischief. "What's to say Jason won't change his mind, too?"

Ming smiled back, but she knew there was a big difference between the two men. Max hadn't found his father trying to kill himself because he was so despondent over the loss of his wife and daughter. And after getting the scoop about how Max and Rachel had met five years earlier, Ming suspected the reason Max had been so down on love and marriage was that he'd already lost his heart to the woman of his dreams.

"I don't know," Ming said. "He's pretty set in his ways. Besides, you weren't around when my engagement to Jason's brother ended. It made me realize that I'm happier on my own."

"Yeah, before Max, I was where you are. All I have to say is that things change." Rachel nudged her chin toward her soon-to-be-sisters-in-law. "Ask either of those two if they believed love was ever going to happen for them. I'll bet both of them felt the way you do right now."

Ming glanced toward the back of the limo, where Emma, nine months pregnant and due any second, and Missy, four months pregnant and radiant, sat side by side, laughing. They had it all. Gorgeous, devoted men. Babies on the way. Envy twisted in Ming's heart.

She sighed. "I'm really happy for all of you, but love doesn't find everyone."

"If you keep an open mind it does."

The big diamond on Rachel's hand sparkled in the low light. Ming stared at it while her fingers combed her hair into three sections. As she braided, she mused that being in love was easy when you were a week away from pairing your engagement ring with a wedding band. Not that she begrudged any of the Case women their happiness. Each one had gone through a lot before finding bliss, none more so than Rachel. But Ming just wasn't in a place where she could feel optimistic about her own chances.

She was in love with a man who refused to let his guard down and allow anyone in, much less her. Because she couldn't get over her feelings for Jason, she'd already lost one man and almost made the biggest mistake of her life. And as of late, she was concerned that having Jason father her child was going to lead to more heartache in the future.

Ming mulled Rachel's words during the second half of the forty-five-minute drive from downtown Houston to the Galveston marina where the men would be waiting. Maybe she should have gone home from the club like Rachel's sister, Hailey, instead of heading out to meet up with Jason. They'd made no plans to rendezvous tonight. She was starting to feel foolish for chasing him all the way out here.

If Jason decided to stay on the yacht with the bachelor party instead of motoring back to the dock on the launch with Max and his brothers, would she be the odd girl out when the couples reunited? Her chest tightened. Ming closed her eyes as they entered the marina parking lot.

The limo came to a stop. Ming heard the door open and the low rumble of male voices. She couldn't make her eyes open. Couldn't face the sight of the three couples embracing while she sat alone and unwanted.

"What's the matter? Did all the dancing wear you out?"

Her eyes flew open at Jason's question. His head and shoulders filled the limo's open door. Heart pounding in delight, she clasped her hands in her lap to keep from throwing herself into his arms. That was not how friends greeted each other.

"I'm not used to having that much fun." She scooted along the seat to the door, accepting Jason's hand as her foot touched the pavement. His familiar cologne mingled with the faint scent of cigars. She wanted to nuzzle her nose into his neck and breathe him in. "How about you? Did you enjoy your strippers?"

"They preferred to be called exotic dancers." He showed her his phone. "They weren't nearly as interesting as this performance."

She gasped at the picture of herself dancing. How had Jason gotten ahold of it? So much for what happens at a bachelorette party stays at a bachelorette party. She eyed the women behind Jason. Who'd ratted her out?

"It was just some guy who asked me to dance," she protested.

"Just some guy?" He kept his voice low, but there was no denying the edge in his tone. "He has his hands all over you."

She enlarged the image, telling herself she was imagining the possessive glint in Jason's eye. "No he doesn't. And if this had been taken five seconds later you would have seen me shove him away and walk off the dance floor."

"Whoa, sounds like a lover's spat to me," Rachel crowed.

Confused by the sparks snapping in Jason's blue eyes, Ming realized a semicircle of couples had formed five feet away. Six faces wore various shades of amusement as they looked on.

Jason composed his expression and turned to face the group. "Not a lover's spat."

"Just a concerned friend," Max intoned, his voice dripping with dry humor.

"Come on, we're all family here." Sebastian's gesture encompassed the whole group. "You can admit to us that you're involved."

"We're not involved." Ming found her voice.

"We're friends," Jason said. "We look out for each other."

"I disagree," Max declared, slapping Jason on the back. "I think you've finally realized that your best friend is the best thing that ever happened to you." He glanced around to see if the others agreed with him. "About time, too."

"You don't know what you're talking about." Jason was making no attempt to laugh off his friend's ribbing.

Ming flinched at Jason's resolute expression. If he'd considered moving beyond friendship, Max would be the one he'd confide in. With Jason's adamant denial, Ming had to face the fact that she was an idiot to hope that Jason might one day realize they belonged together.

"Oh!"

All eyes turned to Emma, who'd bent over, her hand pressed to her round belly.

"Are you okay?" Nathan put his arm around her waist. "Was it a contraction?"

"I don't know. I don't think so." Emma clutched his arm. "Maybe you'd better take me home."

To Ming's delight everyone's focus had shifted to Emma. What might or might not be going on between Ming and Jason was immediately forgotten. As Nathan opened the passenger door for Emma, she looked straight at Ming and winked. Restraining a grin, Ming wondered how many times Emma had used the baby in such a fashion.

"Alone at last," Jason said, drawing her attention back to him. "And the night is still young."

Ming shivered beneath his intense scrutiny. "What did you have in mind?"

"I was thinking maybe you could show me your dancing skills in private."

"Funny. I was thinking maybe you could give me a demonstration of the techniques you picked up from your strippers tonight."

"Exotic dancers," he corrected, opening the passenger door on his car so she could get in. "And I didn't pick up anything because I wasn't anywhere near their dancing."

The last of her tension melted away. "I don't believe you," she teased, keeping her relief hidden. She leaned against his chest and peered up at him from beneath her lashes. "Not so long ago you wouldn't have missed that kind of action."

"Not so long ago I didn't have all the woman I could handle waiting for me at home."

"Except I wasn't waiting for you." Lifting up on tiptoe, she pressed her lips to his and then dropped into the passenger seat.

"No, you were out on the town breaking hearts."

The door shut before her retort reached Jason's ears. Was he really annoyed with her for dancing with someone? Joy flared and died. She was reading too much into it.

"So, where are we heading?" Jason turned out of the marina parking lot and got them headed toward the bridge off the island.

"You may take me home. After all that heartbreaking, my feet are sore." She tried to smile, but her heart hurt too much. "Besides, Muffin is home alone."

"Where's Lily?"

"Supposedly she's out of town this weekend."

"Why supposedly?"

"Because I drove past Evan's house and her car was in the driveway."

"You drove past Evan's house?" Jason shifted his gaze off the road long enough for her to glimpse his alarm. "Are you sure that was a good idea?"

She bristled at his disapproving tone. "I was curious if my sister had lied to me."

"You were curious." He echoed her words doubtfully. "Not bothered that they're together?"

"No."

"Because you two were engaged not that long ago and now he's dating your sister."

"Why do you keep bringing that up?" Her escalating annoyance came through loud and clear. She'd known Jason too long not to recognize when he was picking a fight.

"I want you to be honest with yourself so this doesn't blow up between you and your sister in the future."

"You don't think I'm being honest with myself?"

"Your sister is dating the man who broke off your engagement two weeks before the wedding. I think you're trying too hard to be okay with it."

He took her hand and she was both soothed and frustrated by his touch. No matter what else was happening between them, Jason was her best friend. He knew her better than anyone. Sometimes better than she knew herself. But the warm press of his fingers reminded her that while he could act like a bossy boyfriend, she came up against his defenses every time she started to play girlfriend.

"Right now I've got my hands full with you." Ming wasn't exaggerating on that score. "Can we talk about something else? Please?"

The last thing she wanted was to argue with him when her hopes for the evening required them to be in perfect accord.

"Sure." Even though he agreed, she could tell he wasn't happy about dropping the subject. "What's on your mind?"

"I have the house to myself until late Sunday if you want to hang out."

"That sounds like an invitation to sleep over."

She made a sandwich of his hand and hers and ignored the anxious flutter in her stomach.

"Maybe it is." Flirting with Jason was fun and dangerous. It was easy to lose track of reality and venture into that tricky romantic place best avoided if she wanted their friendship to remain uncomplicated.

Or maybe she was too far gone for things to ever be the same between them again.

The part of her that wanted them to be more than just friends was growing stronger every day. It was a crazy hope, but she couldn't stop the longing any more than Jason could get past his reluctance to fall in love.

"Ming..."

She heard the wariness in his voice and held up her hand. They hadn't spent a single night together this whole week. That had been a mutual decision based on practicality. Neither of them wanted Evan to pop over late one night and find her at Jason's house. Plus, Lily had been in Houston all week and would have noticed if Ming had stayed out all night.

But she was dying to spend the night snuggled in his arms. And the craving had nothing to do with making a baby.

"Forget I said anything." Her breath leaked out in a long, slow sigh. "This past week has been fun. But you and I both know I'm past my prime fertility cycle. It makes no sense for us to keep getting together when I'm either pregnant or I'm too late in my cycle to try."

"Wait. Is that what this week has been about?" He sounded put out. "You're just using me to make a baby?"

Startled, she opened her mouth to deny his claim and realized he was trying to restore their conversation to a lighter note by teasing her. "And a few weeks from now we'll see if you've succeeded." She faked a yawn. "I guess I'm more tired than I thought."

Jason nodded and turned the topic to the bachelorette party. Ming jumped on board, glad to leave behind the tricky path they'd been treading.

By the time he turned the car into her driveway, she'd man-handled her fledgling daydreams about turning their casual sex into something more. She was prepared to say good-night and head alone to her door.

"Call me tomorrow," he told her. "I've got to go shopping for Max and Rachel's wedding present."

"You haven't done that yet?"

"I've been waiting for you to offer to do it for me."

Robbed of a dreamy night in Jason's arms and the pleasure of waking up with him in the morning, Ming let her irrita-tion shine. "You said no about going in on a gift together, so you're on your own."

"Please come shopping with me." He put on his most ap-pealing smile. "You know I'm hopeless when it comes to de-partment stores."

How could she say no when she'd already agreed to help him before they'd started sleeping together. It wasn't fair to treat him differently just because she felt differently toward him.

"What time tomorrow?"

"Eleven? I want to be home to watch the Oilers at three."

"Fine," she grumbled.

With disappointment of her own weighing her down, she plodded up the stairs and let herself into her house. Muffin met her in the foyer. She danced around on her back legs, wring-ing a small smile from Ming's stiff lips.

"I'll take you out back in a second." She waited by the front door long enough to see Jason's headlights retreating down her driveway, then headed toward the French doors that led from her great room to the pool deck.

While the Yorkie investigated the bushes at the back of her property, Ming sat down on a lounge chair and sought the tranquility often gained by sitting beside her turquoise kidney-shaped pool. She revisited her earlier statement to Jason. It made no sense for them to rendezvous each afternoon and have the best sex ever if all they were trying to do was make a baby. Only, if she was completely honest with herself, she'd admit that a baby isn't all she wanted from Jason.

Her body ached with unfulfilled desire. Her soul longed to find the rhythm of Jason's heart beating in time with hers. From the beginning she'd been right to worry that getting intimate with her best friend was going to lead her into trouble. But temptation could be avoided for only so long when all you've ever wanted gets presented to you on a silver platter. She would just have to learn to live with the consequences.

Finding nothing of interest in the shrubbery, Muffin came back to the pool, her nails clicking on the concrete. Sympathetic to her mistress's somber mood, the terrier jumped onto Ming's lap and nuzzled her nose beneath Ming's hand.

"I am such an idiot," she told the dog, rubbing Muffin's head.

"That makes two of us."

Jason hadn't even gotten out of Ming's neighborhood before he'd realized what a huge error he'd made. In fact, he hadn't made it to the end of her block. But just because he'd figured it out didn't mean returning to Ming wasn't an even bigger mistake. So, he'd sat at a stop sign for five minutes, listening to Rascal Flatts and wondering when his life had gotten so damned complicated. Then, he'd turned the car around, used his key to get into Ming's house and found her by the pool.

"Let's go upstairs," he said. "We need to talk."

Ming pulled her hair over one shoulder and began to braid it. "We can't talk here?"

Was she being deliberately stubborn or pretending to be dense?

Without answering, he pivoted on his heel and walked toward the house. Muffin caught up as he crossed the threshold. Behind him, Ming's heels clicked on the concrete as she rushed after him.

"Jason." She sounded breathless and uncertain. She'd stopped in the middle of her kitchen and called after him as he got to the stairs. "Why did you come back?"

Since talking had only created problems between them earlier, he was determined to leave conversation for later. Taking the stairs two at a time, he reached her bedroom in record time. Unfastening his cuffs, he gazed around the room. He hadn't been up here since he'd helped her paint the walls a rich beige. The dark wood furniture, rich chestnut bedspread and touches of sage green gave the room the sophisticated, expensive look of a five-star hotel suite.

"Jason?"

He'd had enough time to unfasten his shirt buttons. Now, as she entered the room, he let the shirt drop off his shoulders and draped it over a chair. "Get undressed."

While she stared at him in confounded silence, he took Muffin from her numb fingers and deposited the dog in the hallway.

"She always sleeps with me," Ming protested as he shut the door.

"Not tonight."

"Well, I suppose she can sleep on Lily's bed. Jason, what's gotten into you?"

His pants joined his shirt on the chair. With only his boxer briefs keeping his erection contained, he set his hands on his hips.

"You and I have been best friends for a long time." Since she wasn't making any effort to slip out of that provocative halter-top and insanely short skirt, he prowled toward her. "And

I've shared with you some of the hardest things I've ever had to go through."

She made no attempt to stop him as he tugged at the thin ribbon holding up her top, but she did grab at the fabric as it began to fall away from her breasts. "If you're saying I know you better than anyone except Max, I'd agree."

Jason hooked his fingers in the top and pulled it from her fingers, exposing her small, perfect breasts. His lungs had to work hard to draw in the air he required. Damn it. They had been together all week, but he still couldn't get over how gorgeous she was, or how much he wanted to mark her as his own.

"Then it seems as if I'm doing our friendship an injustice by not telling you what's going on in my head at the moment."

Reaching around her, he slid down the zipper on her skirt and lowered it past her hips. When it hit the floor, she stepped out of it.

"And what's that?"

Jason crossed his arms over his chest and stared into her eyes. It was nearly impossible to keep his attention from wandering over her mostly naked body. Standing before him in only a black lace thong and four-inch black sandals, she was an exotic feast for the eyes.

"I didn't like seeing you dancing with another man."

The challenge in her almond-shaped eyes faded at his admission. Raw hope rushed in to replace it. "You didn't?"

Jason ground his teeth. He should have been able to contain the truth from her. That he'd admitted to such possessive feelings meant a crack had developed in the well-constructed wall around his heart. But a couple weaknesses in the structure didn't mean he had to demolish the whole thing. He needed to get over his annoyance at her harmless interaction with some random guy. Besides, wasn't he the one who'd initially encouraged her that there was someone out there for her?

To hell with that.

Taking her hand, he drew her toward the bed.

"Not one bit." It reminded him too much of how he'd lost her to his brother. "It looked like you were having fun without me."

"Did it, now?" His confession had restored her confidence. With a sexy smile, she coasted her nails from his chest to the waistband of his underwear. "I guess I was imagining that you were otherwise occupied with your exotic dancers. Did they get you all revved up? Is that why we're here right now?"

He snorted. "The only woman I have any interest in seeing out of her clothes is you."

Heaven help him—it was true. He hadn't even looked at another woman since this business of her wanting to become a mother came up. No. It had been longer than that. Since his brother had broken off their engagement.

The level of desire he felt for her had been eating at him since last weekend when she'd kissed him good-bye at the track. That had been one hell of a parting and if his knee hadn't been so banged up he never would've let her walk away.

This isn't what he'd expected when he'd proposed making love rather than using a clinic to help her conceive. He'd figured his craving for her was strictly physical. That it would wane after his curiosity was satisfied.

What he was feeling right now threatened to alter the temper of their friendship. He should slow things down or stop altogether. Yeah. That had worked great for him earlier. He'd dropped her off and then raced back before he'd gotten more than a couple blocks away.

Frustrated with himself, he didn't give her smug smile a chance to do more than bud before picking her up and dumping her unceremoniously on the bed. Without giving her a chance to recover, he removed first one then the other of her shoes. As each one hit the floor, her expression evolved from surprised to anticipatory.

It drove him crazy how much he wanted her. Every cell in his body ached with need. Nothing in his life had ever compared. Was it knowing her inside and out that made the sexual chemistry between them stronger than normal?

While he snagged her panties and slid them down her pale thighs, she lifted her arms above her head, surrendering herself to his hot gaze. The vision of her splayed across the bed, awaiting his possession, stirred a tremor in his muscles. His hands shook as he dropped his underwear to the floor.

Any thought of taking things slow vanished as she reached for him. A curse made its way past his lips as her confident strokes brought him dangerously close to release.

"Stop." His harsh command sounded desperate.

He took her wrist in a firm grip and pinned it above her head. Lowering himself into the cradle between her thighs, he paused before sliding into her. Two things were eating at him tonight: that picture of her dancing and her preoccupation with Evan and Lily's romance.

"You're mine." The words rumbled out of him like a vow. Claiming her physically hadn't rattled his safe bachelor existence, but this was a whole different story.

"Jason." She waggled her hips and arched her back, trying to entice him to join with her, but although it was close to killing him, he stayed still.

"Say it." With his hands keeping her wrists trapped over her head and his body pinning hers to the mattress, she was at his mercy.

"I can't…" Her eyes went wide with dismay. "…say that."

"Why not?" He rocked against her, giving her a taste of what she wanted.

A groan erupted past her parted lips. She watched him through half-closed eyes. "Because…"

"Say it," he insisted. "And I'll give you what you want."

Her chest rose and fell in shallow, agitated breaths. "What I want…"

He lowered his head and drew circles around her breast with his tongue. His willpower had never felt so strong before. When she'd started dating his brother, he'd been in the worst sort of hell. Deep in his soul, Jason had always believed if she'd choose anyone, she'd pick him. They were best friends. Confidants. Soul mates. And buried where neither had ventured before prom night was a flammable sexual chemistry.

Both of them had been afraid at the power of what existed between them, but he'd been the most vocal about not ruining their friendship. So vocal, in fact, she'd turned to his brother before Jason had had time to come to his senses.

"Mine." He growled the word against her breast as his mouth closed around her nipple.

She gasped at the strong pull of his mouth. "Yours." She wrapped her thighs around his hips. "All yours."

"All mine."

Satisfied, he plunged into her. Locked together, he released her wrists and kissed her hard and deep, sealing her pledge before whisking them both into unheard of pleasure.

Nine

Moving slowly, her legs wobbly from the previous night's exertions, Ming crossed her bedroom to the door, where Muffin scratched and whined. She let the Yorkie in, dipping to catch the small dog before Muffin could charge across the room and disturb the large, naked man sprawled facedown in the middle of the tangled sheets.

"Let's take you outside," she murmured into the terrier's silky coat, tearing her gaze away from Jason.

Still shaken from their passionate lovemaking the night before, she carefully navigated the stairs and headed for the back door. After cuddling against Jason's warm skin all night, the seventy-degree temperature at 7:00 a.m. made her shiver. She should have wrapped more than a silky lavender robe around her naked body.

While Muffin ran off to do her business and investigate the yard for intruders, Ming plopped down on the same lounge she'd occupied the night before and opened her mind to the thoughts she'd held at bay all night long.

What the hell had possessed Jason to demand that she admit to belonging to him? Battling goose bumps, she rubbed at her arms. The morning air brushed her overheated skin but couldn't cool the fire raging inside her. *His.* Even now the word made her muscles tremble and her insides whirl like a leaf caught in a vortex. She dropped her face into her hands and fought the urge to laugh or weep. He made her crazy. First his vow to never fall in love and never get married. Now this.

Muffin barked at something, and Ming looked up to find her dog digging beneath one of the bushes. Normally she'd stop the terrier. Today, she simply watched the destruction happen.

What was she supposed to make of Jason's territorial posturing last night? Why had he reacted so strongly to the inflammatory photo? She'd understand it if they were dating. Then he'd have the right to be angry, to be driven to put his mark on her.

Jason hadn't changed his mind about falling in love. Initially last night he hadn't even wanted to spend the night. So, what had brought him back? It was just about the great sex, right? It wasn't really fair to say he only wanted her body, but he'd shown no interest in accepting her heart.

Ming called Muffin back to the house and started a pot of coffee. She wasn't sure if Jason intended to head home right away or if he would linger. She hoped he'd stick around. She had visions of eating her famous cinnamon raisin bread French toast and drinking coffee while they devoured the Sunday paper. As the day warmed they could go for a swim in her pool. She'd always wanted to make love in the water. Or they could laze in bed. It would be incredible to devote an entire day to hanging out.

Afternoon and evening sex had been more fun and recreational than serious and committed. Ming could pretend they were just enjoying the whole friends-with-benefits experience. Sleeping wrapped in each other's arms had transported them into "relationship" territory. Not to mention the damage done to her emotional equilibrium when Jason admitted to feeling jealous.

She brought logic to bear on last night's events, and squashed the giddy delight bubbling in her heart. She'd strayed a long way from the reason she was in this mess in the first place. Becoming a mom. Time to put things with Jason in perspective. They were friends. Physical intimacy might be messing with their heads at this point, but once she was pregnant all sex would cease and their relationship would go back to being casual and supportive.

"I started coffee," she announced as she stepped into her bedroom and stopped dead at the sight of the person standing by her dresser.

Lily dropped something into Ming's jewelry box and smiled at her sister. "I borrowed your earrings. I hope that's okay."

"It's fine." From her sister, Ming's gaze went straight to the bed and found it empty. Relief shot through her, making her knees wobble. "I thought you were in Portland."

"I came back early."

Since Lily wasn't asking the questions Ming was expecting, she could only assume her sister hadn't run into Jason. "Ah, great."

Where the hell was he?

"How come Jason's car is in the driveway?" Lily asked.

Ming hovered near the doorway to the hall, hoping her sister would take the hint and come with her. "Max's bachelor party was last night. He had a little too much to drink so I drove him home and brought the car back here."

Too late she realized she could have just said he was staying in the guest room. That would at least have given him a reason to be in the house at this hour. Now he was trapped until she could get away from Lily.

Her sister wandered toward the window seat. "I put an offer in on a house."

"Really?" What was going to happen between her and Evan if she was moving away?

Lily plopped down on the cushioned seat and set a pillow in her lap, looking as if she was settling in for a long talk. "You sound surprised."

Ming shot a glance toward the short hallway, flanked by walk-in closets, that led to her bathroom. He had to be in there.

"I guess I was hoping you'd change your mind." She pulled underwear and clothes from her dresser and headed toward the bathroom. "Let me get dressed and then you can tell me all about it."

Her heart thumped vigorously as she shut the bathroom door behind her.

Jason leaned, fully clothed and completely at ease, against her vanity. "I thought you said she was spending the weekend with Evan."

"She was." Ming frowned when she realized he clearly thought she'd lied to him. "Something must have happened. She seems upset." Ming dropped her robe and stepped into her clothes, ignoring his appreciative leer. "Did she see you?"

"I was already dressed and in here when I heard you start talking." Readying himself to make a break for it.

"You were leaving?" Ming shouldn't have been surprised. Last night was over. Time to return their relationship to an easygoing, friendly place. Hadn't she been thinking the same thing? So why did her stomach feel like she'd been eating lead? "Did you intend to say goodbye or just sneak out while I was downstairs with Muffin?"

"Don't be like that."

"Why don't you tell me exactly how I'm supposed to be."

Not wanting her sister to get suspicious, Ming returned to the bedroom without waiting for Jason's answer. Her heart ached, but she refused to give in to the pain pressing on the edge of her consciousness.

Since Lily seemed entrenched in Ming's room, she sat beside her sister on the window seat. To catch Lily's attention, Ming put her hand on her knee. "Tell me about the house."

"House?"

"The one you put an offer in on."

"It's just a house."

"How many bedrooms does it have?"

"Two."

Curious about whatever was plaguing her sister, Ming was distracted by Muffin investigating her way toward the bathroom. "Nice neighborhood?"

"I think I made a huge mistake."

"Then withdraw the offer." She held her breath and waited for the terrier to discover Jason and erupt in a fit of barking.

"Not the house. The guy I've been seeing."

With an effort, Ming returned her full attention to her sister. "I thought you were just friends."

"It's gone a little further than that."

"You're sleeping together?" She asked the question even though she suspected the answer was yes.

Although the fact that her ex-fiancé was dating her sister continued to cause Ming minor discomfort, she was relieved that her strongest emotion was concern for her sister. When jealousy had been her first reaction to the realization that Lily and Evan were involved, Ming had worried that she was turning into a horrible person.

And lately, on top of all her other worries, Ming had started to wonder how Evan would feel if he found out about her and Jason. Something that might just happen if they weren't more careful.

"Yes. But it's not going anywhere."

Ming's gaze strayed to the bathroom door she hadn't completely closed. Muffin had yet to return to the bedroom. What was going on in there?

"Because you don't want it to?"

"I guess."

That tight spot near Ming's heart eased a little. "You guess? Or you know?" When her sister didn't answer, Ming asked, "Do you love him?"

"Yes." Lily stared at her hands.

Ming's throat locked up, but she couldn't blame her sister for falling for Evan. The heart rarely followed a logical path. And it must be tearing Lily apart to love the man who'd almost married her sister.

"I think you should forget about moving to Portland."

"It's not that simple."

Time to rattle her sister's cage a little. "Funny, Jason told me Evan's dating someone, but his situation is complicated, too." Ming gave a little laugh. "Maybe you two should get together and compare notes."

"I suppose we should." Lily gave her a listless smile.

Was there a way for Ming to give her sister permission to have a future with Evan? "You know, I was glad to hear that Evan had found someone and was moving on with his life."

"Really?" Despite Lily's skeptical tone, her eyes were bright with hope.

"He and I weren't mean to be. It happens."

"That's not how you felt six months ago."

"I'm not going to say that having him break off our engagement two weeks before the wedding was any fun, but I'd much rather find out then that we weren't meant to be than to get married and try to make it work only to invest years and then have it fail."

Ming's cell phone rang. She plucked it off the nightstand and answered it before Lily could respond.

"If I'm going to be stuck in your bathroom all morning, I'd love a cup of coffee and some breakfast."

"Good morning to you, too," she said, mouthing Jason's name to Lily. "How are you feeling?"

"Tired and a little aroused after checking out the lingerie drying in your shower."

"Sure, I can return your car." She rolled her eyes in Lily's direction. "Are you sober enough to drive me back here?"

"I guess I don't need to ask what excuse you gave your sister for why my car is at your house." Jason's voice was dry.

"I can follow you over there and bring you back," Lily offered.

"Hey, Lily just offered to follow me to your house so I can drop the car off."

"You're a diabolical woman, do you know that?"

"I'm sure it's no bother," Ming continued. "We're going to make breakfast first though."

"French toast with cinnamon raisin bread?"

"That's right. Your favorite." And one of the few things Ming enjoyed cooking. "Pity you aren't here this morning to have some."

"Just remember that paybacks can be painful."

"Oh, I didn't realize you needed your car to go shopping for Max and Rachel's wedding gift this morning. I'll see you in fifteen minutes." She disconnected the call. "I'm going to run Jason's car over to him and then I'll come back and we can make breakfast."

"Are you sure you don't want me to drive you over there?"

"No. I think the fresh air will do him some good."

She escorted Lily to the kitchen and settled her with a cup of green tea before she headed for the front door. Jason was already in the car when she arrived.

"Lily sounded upset this morning," Jason said. "Did I hear her say she put an offer on a house?"

"In Portland. But she seems really unsure what her next move is." She drove the car into the parking lot of a coffee shop in her neighborhood and cut the engine. "She's conflicted about going." She paused a beat. "Did you know they're sleeping together?"

Silence filled the space between her and Jason. Ming listened to the engine tick as it cooled, her thoughts whirling.

"Yes." He was keeping things from her. That wasn't like him.

"And you didn't tell me?"

"I didn't want you to get upset."

"I'm not upset." Not about Lily and Evan.

Last weekend she'd discovered what she really wanted from Jason. It wasn't a baby she would raise on her own. It was a husband who'd adore her and a bunch of kids to smother with love. She was never going to have that with him, and accepting that was tearing her apart.

"Well, you don't look happy."

"I want my sister to stay in Houston." The air inside the car became stuffy and uncomfortable. Ming shoved open the door and got out.

By the time she reached the Camaro's front bumper, Jason was there, waiting for her. "What happens if Lily and Evan decide to get married?"

Then she would be happy for them. "Evan and I were over six months ago."

"You and Evan broke up six months ago."

"Are you insinuating I'm not over him?"

"Are you?" He set his hand on his hips, preventing her from going past.

"Don't be ridiculous." She tried to sidestep him, but he shifted to keep her blocked. "Would I be sleeping with you if I was hung up on your brother?"

"If I recall, the only reason you're sleeping with me is so you can get pregnant."

She should be relieved that he believed that. It alleviated the need for complicated explanations. But what had happened between them meant so much more to her than that she couldn't stay silent.

"Perhaps you need to think a little harder about that first afternoon in your kitchen." She leaned into his body, surrendering her pride. "Did it seem as if all I was interested in was getting pregnant?"

"Ming." The guilt in his voice wrenched at her. He cupped her shoulders, the pressure comforting, reassuring.

She stared at his chest and hoped he wouldn't see the tears burning her eyes. "I knew it was going to get weird between us."

"It's not weird."

"It's weird." She circled around him and headed to the passenger side. "I should probably get back."

For a moment Jason stood where she'd left him. Ming watched him through the windshield, appreciating the solitude to collect her thoughts. It was her fault that their relationship was strained. If she'd just stuck with her plan and used a clinic to get pregnant, she wouldn't have developed a craving for a man who could never be hers. And she wouldn't feel miserable for opening herself to love.

As Jason slid behind the wheel, she composed her expression and gathered breath to tell him that they needed to go back to being friends without benefits, but he spoke first.

"Last night." He gripped the steering wheel hard and stared straight ahead. "I crossed the line."

To fill the silence that followed his confession, Jason started the Camaro, but for once the car's powerful engine didn't make him smile.

"Because of what you wanted me to say." Ming sounded irritated and unsure.

"Yes." Moments earlier, he'd considered skirting the truth, but she'd been honest about her feelings toward him.

"Then why did you?"

Making love to her had flipped a switch, lighting him up like a damned merry-go-round. He kept circling, his thoughts stuck on the same track, going nowhere. He liked that they were lovers. At the same time he relied on the stability of their friendship. So far he'd been operating under the belief that he could have it both ways. Now, his emotions were getting away from him. Logic told him lust and love were equally powerful and easily confused. But he'd begun to question his determination to never fall in love.

"Because it's how I feel."

"And that's a bad thing?"

He saw the hope in her eyes and winced. "It isn't bad. We've been close a long time. My feelings for you are strong." How did he explain himself without hurting her? "I just don't want to lead you on and I think that's what I did."

"Lead me on?" She frowned. "By making me think that you wanted to move beyond friendship into something…more?" Her fingers curled into fists. "I'm not sure who I'm more angry with right now. You or me."

If he'd known for sure that sleeping with her would complicate their friendship, would he have suggested it? Yes. Even now he wasn't ready to go back to the way things were. He had so much he longed to explore with Ming.

If he was honest with himself, he'd admit that helping her get pregnant was no longer his primary motivation for continuing their intimate relationship. He'd have to weigh a deeper connection with Ming against the risk that someday one of them would wake up and realize they were better off as friends. If emotions were uneven, their friendship might not survive.

"Do you want to stop?" He threw the car into gear and backed out of the parking spot.

"You're making me responsible for what does or doesn't happen between us? How is that fair?"

Below her even tone was a cry for help. Jason wanted to pull her close and kiss away her frown. If today they agreed to go back to the way things were, how long would he struggle against the impulse to touch her the way a lover would?

"I want you to be happy," he told her. "Whatever that takes."

"Do you?" She looked skeptical. "Last night I wanted you to stay, but you got all tense and uncomfortable." A deep breath helped get her voice back under control. When she continued, she seemed calmer. "I know it's because you have a rule against spending the night with the women you see."

"But I spent last night with you."

"And this morning you couldn't put your clothes on fast enough." She stared at him hard enough to leave marks on his face.

"So what do you want from me?"

"I'd like to know what you want. Are we just friends? Are we lovers?"

Last night he'd denied their relationship to his friends and felt resistance to her suggestion that he stay the night with her. As happy as Max and his brothers were to be in love with three terrific women, Jason could only wonder about future heart-break when he looked at the couples. He didn't want to live with the threat of loss hanging over his head, but he couldn't deny that the thought of Ming with another man bugged him. So did her dismay that Evan had fallen in love with Lily.

"I won't deny that I think we're good together," he said. "But you know how I feel about falling in love."

"You don't want to do it."

"Can't we just keep enjoying what we have? You know I'll always be there for you. The chemistry between us is terrific. Soon you'll be busy being a mom and won't have time for me." He turned the car into her driveway and braked but didn't put the Camaro in Park. He needed to get away, to mull over what they'd talked about today. "Let's have dinner tomorrow."

"I can't. It's the Moon Festival. Lily and I are having dinner with our parents tomorrow. I'm going to tell them my decision to have a baby, and she's going to tell them she's moving." Ming sighed. "We promised to be there to support each other."

Jason didn't envy either sister. Helen Campbell was a stubborn, opinionated woman who believed she knew what was best for her daughters. At times, Ming had almost collapsed beneath the weight of her mother's hopes and dreams for her.

She hadn't talked about it, but Jason knew the breakup of her engagement had been a major blow to Ming's mother.

"What about Tuesday?" he suggested.

She put her hand on the door release, poised to flee. "It's going to be a hectic week with Max and Rachel's wedding next weekend."

Jason felt a sense of loss, but he didn't understand why. He and Ming were still friends. Nothing about that had changed.

"What's wrong?"

"It's too much to go into now."

Jason caught her arm as she pushed the door open and prevented her from leaving. "Wait."

Ming made him act in ways that weren't part of his normal behavior. Today, for example. He'd hid in her bathroom for fifteen minutes while she and her sister had occupied the bedroom. There wasn't another woman on earth he would have done that for.

Now he was poised to do something he'd avoided with every other woman he'd been involved with. "You're obviously upset. Tell me what's going on."

"I feel like an idiot." Her voice was thick with misery. "These last couple weeks with you have been fantastic and I've started thinking of us as a couple."

Her admission didn't come as a complete shock. Occasionally over the years he too had considered what they'd be like together. She knew him better than anyone. He'd shared with her things no one else knew. His father's suicide attempt. How he'd initially been reluctant to join the family business. The fact that the last words he'd spoken to his little sister before she'd died had been angry ones.

"Even knowing how you feel about love—" She stopped speaking and blinked rapidly. "Turns out I'm just like all those other women you've dated. No, I'm worse, because I knew better and let myself believe…" Her chin dropped toward her chest. "Forget it, okay?"

Was she saying she was in love with him? Her declaration hit him like a speeding truck. He froze, unable to think, unsure what to feel. Had she lost her mind? Knowing he wasn't built for lasting relationships, she'd opened herself up to heartbreak?

And where did they go from here? He couldn't ask her to continue as they'd been these past two weeks. But he'd never had such mind-blowing chemistry with anyone before, and he was a selfish bastard who wasn't going to give that up without a fight.

"Saturday night, after the wedding, we're going to head to my house and talk. We'll figure out together what to do." But he suspected the future was already written. "Okay?"

"There's nothing to figure out." She slid out of the car. "We're friends. Nothing is going to change that."

But as he watched her head toward her front door, Jason knew in the space of a few minutes, everything had changed.

Ten

Ming caught her sister wiping sweaty palms on her denim-clad thighs as she stopped the car in front of her parents' house and killed the engine. She put her hand over Lily's and squeezed in sympathy.

"We'll be okay if we stick together."

Arm in arm they headed up the front walk. No matter what their opinions were about each other's decisions, Ming knew they'd always form a unified front when it came to their mother.

Before they reached the front door, it opened and a harlequin Great Dane loped past the handsome sixty-year-old man who'd appeared in the threshold.

"Dizzy, you leave that poor puppy alone," Patrick Campbell yelled, but his words went unheeded as Dane and Ming's Yorkie raced around the large front yard.

"Dad, Muffin's fine." In fact, the terrier could run circles around the large dog and dash in for a quick nip then be gone again before Dizzy knew what hit her. "Let them run off a little energy."

After surviving rib-bruising hugs from their father, Ming and Lily captured the two dogs and brought them inside. The house smelled like heaven, and Ming suspected her mother had spent the entire weekend preparing her favorite dishes as well as the special moon cakes.

Ming sat down at her parents' dining table and wondered how the thing didn't collapse under the weight of all the food. She'd thought herself too nervous to eat, but once her plate was heaped with a sample of everything, she began eating with relish. Lily's appetite didn't match hers. She spent most of the meal staring at her plate and stabbing her fork into the food.

After dinner, they took their moon cakes outside to eat beneath the full moon while their mother told them the story of how the festival came to be.

"The Mongolians ruled China during the Yuan Dynasty," Helen Campbell would begin, her voice slipping naturally into storytelling rhythm. She was a professor at the University of Houston, teaching Chinese studies, language and literature. "The former leaders from the Sung dynasty wanted the foreigners gone, but all plans to rebel were discovered and stopped. Knowing that the Moon Festival was drawing near, the rebel leaders ordered moon cakes to be baked with messages inside, outlining the attack. On the night of the Moon Festival, the rebels successfully overthrew the government. What followed was the establishment of the Ming dynasty. Today, we eat the moon cakes to remember."

No matter how often she heard the tale, Ming never grew tired of it. As a first-generation American on her mother's side, Ming appreciated the culture that had raised her mother. Although as children both Ming and Lily had fought their mother's attempts to keep them attached to their Chinese roots, by the time Ming graduated from college, she'd become fascinated with China's history.

She'd visited China over a dozen times when Helen had returned to Shanghai, where her family still lived. Despite growing up with both English and Chinese spoken in the house, Ming had never been fluent in Mandarin. Thankfully her Chinese relatives were bilingual. She couldn't wait to introduce her own son or daughter to her Chinese family.

Stuffed to the point where it was difficult to breathe, Ming sipped jasmine tea and watched her sister lick sweet bean paste off her fingers. The sight blended with a hundred other memories of family and made her smile.

"I've decided to have a baby," she blurted out.

After her parents exchanged a look, Helen set aside her plate as if preparing to do battle.

"By yourself?"

Ming glanced toward Lily, who'd begun collecting plates. Ever since they'd been old enough to reach the sink, it was understood that their mother would cook and the girls would clean up.

"It's not the way I dreamed of it happening, but yes. By myself."

"I know how much you want children, but have you thought everything through?" Her mother's lips had thinned out of existence.

"Helen, you know she can handle anything she sets her mind to," her father said, ever supportive.

Ming leaned forward in her chair and looked from one parent to the other. "I'm not saying it's going to be a picnic, but I'm ready to be a mom."

"A single mom?" Helen persisted.

"Yes."

"You know my thoughts on this matter." Her mother's gaze grew keen. "How does Jason feel about what you're doing?"

Ming stared at the flowers that surrounded her parents' patio. "He's happy for me."

"He's a good man," her mother said, her expression as tranquil as Ming had ever seen it. "Are you hoping he'll help you?"

"I don't expect him to." Ming wondered if her mother truly

understood that she was doing this on her own. "He's busy with his own life."

Patrick smiled. "I remember how he was with your cousins. He's good with kids. I always thought he'd make a great father."

"You did?" The conversation had taken on a surreal quality for Ming. Since he never intended to get married, she'd never pictured Jason as a father. But now that her dad had mentioned it, she could see Jason relishing the role.

"What I meant about Jason…is he going to help you make the baby?" her mother interjected.

"Why would you think that?"

"You two are close. It seems logical."

Ming kept her panic off her face, but it wasn't easy. "It would mess up our friendship."

"Why? I'm assuming you're going to use a clinic."

This was all hitting a little too close to home. "That's what I figured I'd do." Until Jason came up with the crazy notion of them sleeping together. "I'd better give Lily a hand in the kitchen."

Leaving her parents to process what she'd told them, Ming sidled up to her sister.

"I shared my news." She started rinsing off dishes and stacking them in the dishwasher. "Are you going to tell them you've bought a house in Portland?"

"I changed my mind."

"About the house or Portland?"

"Both."

"Evan must be thrilled." The words slipped out before Ming realized what she was saying. In her defense, she was rattled by her father's speculation about Jason being a great dad and her mother's guess that he was going to help her get pregnant.

"Evan?" Lily tried to sound confused rather than anxious, but her voice buckled beneath the weight of her dismay. "Why would Evan care?"

The cat was out of the bag. Might as well clear the air. "Because you two are dating?"

Ming was aware that keeping a secret about her and Jason while unveiling her sister's love life was the most hypocritical thing she'd done in months.

"Don't be ridiculous."

"Evan admitted it to Jason and he told me."

"I'm sorry I didn't tell you."

"Don't you think you should have?" She didn't want to resent Lily for finding happiness.

"I honestly didn't think anything was going to happen between us."

"Happen between you when, exactly?" Ming's frustration with her own love life was bubbling to the surface. "The first time you went out? The first time he kissed you?"

"I don't want this to come between us."

"Me, either." But at the moment it was, and Ming couldn't dismiss the resentment rumbling through her.

"But I don't want to break up with him." Beneath Lily's determined expression was worry. "I can't."

Shock zipped across Ming's nerve endings. "Is it that serious?"

"He told me he loves me."

"Wow." Ming exhaled in surprise.

It had taken almost a year of dating for Evan to admit such deep feelings for her. As reality smacked her in the face, she was overcome by the urge to curl into a ball and cry her eyes out. What was wrong with her? She wasn't in love with Evan. She'd made her peace with their breakup. Why couldn't she be happy for her sister?

"Do you feel the same?"

Lily wouldn't meet her gaze. "I do."

"How long have you been going out?"

"A couple months. I know it seems fast, but I've been interested in Evan since high school. Until recently, I had no idea he saw me as anything more than your baby sister. Emphasis on the *baby*." Lily's lips curved down at the corners.

There was a five-year difference in their ages. That gap would have seemed less daunting as Lily moved into her twenties and became a successful career woman.

"I guess he's seen the real you at last."

"I want you to know, I never meant for this to happen."

"Of course you didn't."

"It's just that no one has control over who they fall in love with."

What Lily had just told Ming should have relieved her own guilt over what she and Jason were doing. Evan had moved on. He was in love. If he ever discovered what was happening between her and Jason, Evan should be completely accepting. After all, he'd fallen for her sister. All Ming was doing was getting pregnant with Jason's child. It wasn't as if they were heading down the path to blissfully-ever-after.

Struck by the disparity between the perfect happiness of every couple she knew and the failure of her own love life, Ming's heart ached. Her throat closed as misery battered her. Her longing for a man she could never have and her inability to let him go trapped her. It wasn't enough to have Jason as her best friend. She wanted to claim him as her lover and the man she'd spend the rest of her life committed to. On her current path, Ming wasn't sure how she was ever going to find her way out of her discontent, but since she wasn't the sort who moldered in self-pity, she'd better figure it out.

Unwinding in her office after a hectic day of appointments, Ming rechecked the calendar where she'd been keeping track of her fertility cycle for the past few months. According to her history, her period should have started today.

Excitement raced through her. She could be pregnant. For a second she lost the ability to breathe. Was she ready for this? Months of dreaming and hoping for this moment hadn't prepared her for the reality of the change in her life between one heartbeat and the next.

Ming stared at her stomach. Did Jason's child grow inside her? She caught herself mid-thought. This was her child. Not hers and Jason's. She had to stop fooling herself that they were going to be a family. She and Jason were best friends who wanted very different things out of life. They were not a couple. Never would be.

"Are you still here?" Terry leaned into the room and flashed his big white smile. "I thought you had a wedding rehearsal to get to."

Ming nodded. "I'm leaving in ten minutes. The church is only a couple miles away."

"Did those numbers I gave you make you feel better or worse?"

Earlier in the week Terry had opened up the practice's books so she could see all that went into the running of the business. Although part of her curriculum at dental school had involved business courses that would help her if she ever decided to open her own practice, her college days were years behind her.

"I looked them over, but until I get Jason to walk me through everything, I'm still feeling overwhelmed."

"Understandable. Let me know if you have any questions."

After Terry left, Ming grabbed her purse and headed for the door. Until five minutes ago, she'd been looking forward to this weekend. Max and Rachel were a solid couple.

Thanks to Susan Case, Max's mother, the wedding promised to be a magical event. After both Nathan and Sebastian had skipped formal ceremonies—Nathan marrying Emma on a Saint Martin beach and Sebastian opting for an impromptu Las Vegas elopement—Susan had threatened Max with bodily harm if she was denied this last chance at a traditional wedding.

Most brides would have balked at so much input from their future mother-in-law, but Rachel's only family was her sister, and Ming thought the busy employment agency owner appreciated some of the day-to-day details being handled by Max's mother.

When Ming arrived at the church, most of the wedding party was already there. She set her purse in the last pew and let her gaze travel up the aisle to where the minister was speaking to Max. As the best man, Jason stood beside him, listening intently. Ming's breath caught at the sight of him clad in a well-cut dove-gray suit, white shirt and pale green tie.

Was she pregnant? It took effort to keep her fingers from wandering to her abdomen. When she'd embarked on this journey three weeks ago, she'd expected that achieving her goal would bring her great joy and confidence. Joy was there, but it was shadowed by anxiety and doubt.

She wasn't second-guessing her decision to become a mom, but she no longer wanted to do it alone. Jason would freak out if he discovered how much she wanted them to be a real family. Husband, wife, baby. But that's not how he'd visualized his future, and she had no right to be disappointed that they wanted different things.

As if her troubled thoughts had reached out to him, Jason glanced in her direction. When their eyes met, some of her angst eased. Raising his eyebrows, he shot her a crooked grin. Years of experience gave her insight into exactly what he was thinking.

Max couldn't be talked out of this crazy event.

She pursed her lips and shook her head.

You shouldn't even try. He's found his perfect mate.

"Are you two doing that communicating-without-words thing again?"

Ming hadn't noticed Missy stop beside her. With her red hair and hazel eyes, Sebastian's wife wore chocolate brown better than anyone Ming had ever met.

"I guess we are." Ming's gaze returned to Jason.

"Have you ever thought about getting together? I know you

were engaged to his brother and all, but it seems as if you'd be perfect for each other."

"Not likely." Ming had a hard time summoning energy to repeat the tired old excuses. She was stuck in a rut where Jason was concerned, with no clue how to get out. "We're complete opposites."

"No one is more different than Sebastian and I." Missy grinned. "It can be a lot of fun."

Based on the redhead's saucy smile, Ming had little trouble imagining just how much fun the newlyweds were having. She sighed. Prior conversations with Emma, Missy and Rachel had shown her that not everyone's road to romance was straight and trouble-free, but Ming knew she wasn't even on a road with Jason. More like a faint deer trail through the woods.

"He doesn't want to fall in love."

Missy surveyed the three Case men as the minister guided them into position near the front of the church. "So make him."

Rather than lecture Missy about how hopeless it was to try changing Jason's mind about love and marriage, Ming clamped her lips together and forced a smile. What good would it do to argue with a newly married woman who was a poster child for happily ever after?

As she practiced her walk up the aisle on Nathan's arm, she had a hard time focusing on the minister's instructions. Casting surreptitious glances at Jason, standing handsome and confident beside Max, she fought against despair as she realized there would never be a day when the man she loved waited for her at the front of the church. She would never wear an elegant gown of white satin and shimmering pearls and speak the words that would bind them together forever.

"And then you separate, each going to your place." The minister signaled to the organist. "Here the music changes to signal that the bride is on her way."

While everyone watched Rachel float up the aisle, her happiness making it appear as if her feet didn't touch the ground,

Ming stared down at the floor and fought against the tightness in her throat. She was going to drive herself mad pining for an ending that could never be.

Twenty minutes later, the wedding party was dismissed. They trooped back down the aisle, two-by-two, with Nathan and Ming bringing up the rear.

"How's Emma doing?" she asked. Nathan's wife was five days past her due date.

"She's miserable." Nathan obviously shared his wife's discomfort. "Can't wait for the baby to come."

"I didn't see her. Is she here tonight?"

"No." A muscle jumped in his jaw. "I told her to stay home and rest up. Tomorrow is going to be a long day." Nathan scowled. "But if I know her, she's working on the last of her orders to get them done before the baby arrives."

Nathan's wife made some of the most unique and beautiful jewelry Ming had ever seen. Missy's wedding set was one of her designs. From what Jason had told her, Max and Rachel's wedding rings had been created by Emma as well.

"I'm worried she's not going to slow down even after the baby arrives," Nathan continued, looking both exasperated and concerned. "She needs to take better care of herself."

"Why, when she has you to take care of her?"

Nathan gave her a wry grin. "I suppose you're right. See you tomorrow."

Smiling thoughtfully at Nathan's eagerness to get home to his wife, Ming went to fetch her purse. When she straightened, she discovered Jason standing beside her. He slipped his fingers through hers and squeezed gently.

"I missed you this week."

Shivers danced along her spine at his earnest tone. "I missed you, too."

More than she cared to admit. Although they'd talked every day on the phone, their conversations had revolved around the dental practice financials and other safe topics. They hadn't discussed that Evan was in love with Lily, and Ming wasn't sure Jason even knew.

"I don't suppose I could talk you into coming home with me tonight," he murmured, drawing her after the departing couples.

Although tempted by his offer, she shook her head. "I promised Lily we'd hang out, and I have an early appointment to get my hair and makeup done tomorrow." She didn't like making up excuses, but after what she'd started to suspect earlier, the only thing she wanted to do was take the pregnancy test she'd bought on the way to the church and see if it was positive. "Tomorrow after the reception."

Jason walked her to her car and held her door while she got behind the wheel. He lingered with his hand on the door. The silence between them grew heavy with expectation. Ming's heart slowed. The crease between his brows told her that something troubled him.

She was the first to break the silence. "Evan's in love with Lily and she's decided to stay in Houston."

"How do you feel about that?"

"I'm thrilled."

"I mean about how Evan feels about her."

With a determined smile she shook her head. "I'm happy for him and Lily."

"You're really okay with it?"

"I'm going to be a mom. That's what I'm truly excited about. That's where I need to put all my energy."

"Because you know I'm here if you want to talk."

"Really, I'm fine," she said, keeping her voice bright and untroubled. She knew he was just being a good friend, but she couldn't stop herself from wishing his concern originated in the same sort of love she felt for him. "See you at the restaurant."

He stared at her for a long moment more before stepping back. "Save me a seat."

And with that, he closed her car door.

Eleven

Jason had never been so glad to be done with an evening. Sitting beside Ming while toast after toast had been made to the bride and groom, he'd never felt more alone. But it's what he wanted. A lifetime with no attachments. No worries that he'd ever become so despondent over losing a woman that he'd want to kill himself.

Logic and years of distance told him that his father had been in an extremely dark place after the death of his wife and daughter. But there was no reason to believe that Jason would ever suffer such a devastating loss. And if he did, wasn't he strong enough to keep from sinking into a hole and never coming out?

And yet, his reaction to that photo of her dancing hadn't exactly been rational. Neither had the way he'd demanded that she declare herself to be his. Oh, he'd claimed that he didn't want to lead her on. The truth was he was deathly afraid of losing her.

"I'm heading home." Ming leaned her shoulder against his.

Her breath brushed his neck with intoxicating results. "Can you walk me to my car?"

"I think I'll leave, too." The evening was winding down. Sebastian and Missy had already departed.

As soon as they cleared the front door, he took her hand. Funny how such a simple act brought him so much contentment. "Did I mention you look beautiful tonight?"

"Thank you." Only her eyes smiled at him. The rest of her features were frozen into somber lines.

They reached her car and before he could open her door, she put a hand on his arm. "This is probably not the best place for this…" She glanced around, gathered a breath and met his gaze. Despite her tension, joy glittered in her dark eyes. "I'm pregnant."

Her declaration crushed the air from his lungs. He'd been expecting it, but somehow now, knowing his child grew inside her, he was beyond thrilled.

"You're sure?"

"As sure as an early pregnancy test can be." Her fingers bit into his arm. "I took one at the restaurant." She laughed unsteadily. "How crazy is that? I couldn't even wait until I got home."

Jason wrapped his arms around her and held her against him. A baby. Their baby. He wanted to rush back into the restaurant and tell everyone. They were going to be parents. Reality penetrated his giddy mood. Except she didn't want to share the truth with anyone. She intended to raise the child on her own.

"I'm glad you couldn't wait," he told her, his words muffled against her hair. "It's wonderful news."

From chest to thigh, her long, lean body was aligned with his. How many months until holding her like this he'd feel only her rounded stomach? Or would he even get to snuggle with her, her head resting on his shoulder, her arms locked around his waist?

"Of course, this means…"

Knowing what was coming next, Jason growled. "You aren't seriously going to break up with me on the eve of Max's wedding."

"Break up with you?" She tipped her head back so he could see her smile, but she wouldn't meet his eyes. "That would require us to be dating."

But they'd sworn never to explore that path. Would they miss a chance to discover that the real reason they were such good friends was because they were meant to be together?

Are you listening to yourself? What happened to swearing you'd never fall in love?

Frustrated by conflicting desires, Jason's hold on her tightened. Her breath hitched as he lowered his head and claimed her mouth. Heat flared between them. Their tongues tangled while delicious sensations licked at his nerves. She was an endless feast for his senses. A balm for his soul. She challenged him and made him a better person. And now she was pregnant with his child. They could be happy together.

All he needed to do was let her in.

He broke off the kiss and dragged his lips across her cheek. What existed in his heart was hers alone. He could tell her and change everything.

The silence between them lengthened. Finally, Ming slid her palm down his heaving chest and stepped back.

"We're just good friends who happen to be sleeping together until one of us got pregnant," she said, her wry tone at odds with her somber eyes.

"And we promised nothing would get in the way of our friendship."

She sagged against him. "And it won't."

"Not ever."

Our baby.

Jason's words the previous night had given her goose bumps.

Almost ten hours later, Ming rubbed her arms as the sensation lingered.

My baby.

She tried to infuse the declaration with conviction, but couldn't summon the strength. Not surprising, when his claim filled her with unbridled joy. It was impossible to be practical when her heart was singing and she felt lighter than air.

Pulling into the parking lot of the salon Susan Case had selected based on their excellent reputation, Ming spent a few minutes channeling her jubilation over her baby news into happiness for Rachel and Max. It was easy to do.

The bride was glowing as she chatted with her sister, Hailey, Missy and Susan. As Ming joined the group, two stylists took charge of Rachel, escorting her to a chair near the back. Rachel had let her hair grow out from the boyish cut she'd had when Ming had first met her. For her wedding look, the stylists pinned big loops of curls all over her head and attached tiny white flowers throughout.

Unaccustomed to being the center of attention, Rachel endured being fussed over with good grace. Watching the stylists in action, Ming was certain the bride would be delighted with the results.

Because all the bridesmaids had long hair, they were styled with the front pulled away from their face and soft waves cascading down their back. When the four girls lined up so Susan could take a photo, the resulting picture was feminine and romantic.

Although the wedding wasn't until four, the photographer was expecting them to be at the church, dressed in their wedding finery by one. With a hundred or more photos to smile for and because she'd skipped breakfast after oversleeping, Ming decided she'd better grab lunch before heading to the church. She ended up being the last to arrive.

Naturally her gaze went straight to Jason. Standing halfway up the aisle, model-gorgeous in his tuxedo, he looked far more stressed than the groom. Ming flashed back to their senior prom, the evening that marked the beginning of the end for her in terms of experiencing true love.

"Don't you look handsome," she exclaimed as he drew near. Over the years, she'd had a lot of practice pretending she wasn't infatuated with him. That stood her in good stead as Jason pulled her into his arms for a friendly hug.

"You smell as edible as you look," he murmured. "Whose insane idea was it to dress you in a color that made me want to devour you?"

For her fall wedding, Rachel had chosen strapless empire waist bridesmaid dresses in muted apple green. They would all be carrying bouquets of orange, yellow and fuchsia.

Ming quivered as his sexy voice rumbled through her. If he kept staring at her with hungry eyes, she might not be able to wait until after the wedding to get him alone. A deep breath helped Ming master her wayward desires. Today was about Max and Rachel.

"Susan proposed apple green, I believe." She'd never know how she kept her tone even given the chaos of her emotions.

"Remind me to thank her later."

Ming restrained a foolish giggle and pushed him to arm's length so she could check him out in turn. "I like you in a tux. You should wear one more often."

"If I'd known how much fun it would be to have you undress me with your eyes, I would have done so sooner."

"I'm not undressing—" She stopped the flow of words as Emma waddled within earshot.

"I don't know what you're planning on taking off," the very pregnant woman said as she stepped into the pew beside them, "but I'd start with what he's wearing."

Jason smirked at Ming, but there was no time for her to respond because the photographer's assistant called for the wedding party to come to the front of the church.

With everyone in a festive mood, it was easy for Ming to

laugh and joke with the rest of Rachel's attendants as they posed for one photo after another. The photographer's strict schedule allowed little time for her to dwell on how close she'd been to her own wedding six months earlier, or whether she might be in this same position months from now if things continued to progress with Lily and Evan.

But in the half-hour lull between photos and ceremony, she had more than enough quiet to contemplate what might have been for her and to ponder the future.

She kept apart from the rest of the group, not wanting her bout of melancholy to mar the bride and groom's perfect day. Shortly before the ceremony was supposed to start, Jason approached her and squeezed her hand.

"You look pensive."

"I was just thinking about the baby."

"Me, too." His expression was grave. "I want to tell everyone I'm the father."

Ming's heart convulsed. Last night, after discovering she was pregnant, she'd longed to stand at Jason's side and tell everyone they were having a baby. Of course, doing it would bring up questions about whether or not they were together.

"Are you sure this is a good idea?"

"The only reason you wanted to keep quiet was because you didn't want to hurt Evan. But he's moved on with your sister."

"So you decided this because Evan and Lily are involved?"

"It isn't about them. It's about us. I'm going to be in the child's life on a daily basis." His expression was more determined than she'd ever seen it. "I think I should be there as his dad rather than as Uncle Jason."

He'd said *us*.

Only it wasn't about her and Jason. Not in the way she wanted. Ming's heart shuddered like a damaged window battered by strong winds. At any second it could shatter into a thousand pieces. She loved the idea that he wanted to be a father, but she couldn't ignore her yearning to have him be there for her as well.

"Come on, you two," Missy called as the wedding party began moving into position near the church's inner door. "We're on."

Jason strode to his position in line and Ming relaxed her grip on her bouquet before the delicate stems of the Gerber daisies snapped beneath the intensity of her conflicting emotions.

As maid of honor, Rachel's sister, Hailey, was already in place behind Max and his parents. The music began signaling the trio to start down the aisle. The groom looked relaxed and ready as he accompanied his parents to their places at the front of the church.

The bright flowers in Ming's hands quivered as she stood beside Nathan. He appeared on edge. His distress let Ming forget about her own troubles.

"Are you okay?" she asked.

Lines bracketed his mouth. "I tried to convince Emma to stay home. Although she wouldn't admit it, she's really having a difficult time today. I'm worried about her."

"I'm sure it's natural to be uncomfortable when you're past your due date," Ming said and saw immediately that her words had little effect on the overprotective father-to-be. "She'll let you know if anything is wrong."

"I'm concerned that she won't." He glanced behind him at the bride. "She didn't want anything to disturb your day."

Rachel put her hand on Nathan's arm, her expression sympathetic. "I appreciate both of you being here today, but if you think she needs to be at home, take her there right after the ceremony."

Nathan leaned down and grazed Rachel's cheek with his lips. "I will. Thank you."

He seemed marginally less like an overwound spring as they took their turn walking down the aisle. It might have helped that his wife beamed at him from the second row. Ming's stom ach twisted in reaction to their happiness. Even for someone who wasn't newly pregnant and madly in love with a man who refused to feel the same way, it was easy to get overwhelmed by emotions at a wedding. Holding herself together became easier as she watched Rachel start down the aisle.

The bride wore a long strapless dress unadorned by beading or lace. Diamond and pearl earrings were her only jewelry. Her styling was romantic and understated, allowing the bride's beauty and her utter happiness to shine.

With her father dead and her mother out of her life since she was four, Rachel had no one to give her away. Ming's sadness lasted only until she realized this was the last time Rachel would walk alone. At the end of the ceremony, she would be Max's wife and part of his family.

Ming swallowed past the lump in her throat as the minister began talking. The rest of the ceremony passed in a blur. She was roused out of her thoughts by the sound of clapping. Max had swept Rachel into a passionate kiss. The music began once more and the happy couple headed back down the aisle, joined for life.

Because they'd been the last up the aisle, Nathan and Ming were the last to return down it. They didn't get far, however. As they drew near Emma, Ming realized something was wrong. Nathan's wife was bending forward at the waist and in obvious pain. When Nathan hastened to her side, she clutched his forearm and leaned into his strength.

"I think it might be time to get to the hospital," she said, her brown eyes appearing darker than ever in her pale face.

"How long has this been going on?" he demanded.

"Since this morning."

Nathan growled.

"I'm fine. I wanted both of us to be here for Rachel and Max. And now I'd like to go to the hospital and give birth to our son."

"Stubborn woman," Nathan muttered as he put a supporting arm around his wife and escorted her down the aisle.

"Do you want us to come with you?" Max's mother asked, following on their heels. She reached her hand back to her husband.

"No." Emma shook her head. "Stay and enjoy the party. The baby probably won't come anytime soon." But as she said it, another contraction stopped her in her tracks.

"I'm going to get the car." Handing his wife off to Ming, Nathan raced out of the church.

Ming and Emma continued their slow progress.

"Has he always been like this?" Ming asked, amused and ever so envious.

"It all started when my father decided to make marrying me part of a business deal Nathan was doing with Montgomery Oil. Since then he's got this crazy idea in his head that I need to be taken care of."

"I think it's sweet."

Emma's lips moved into a fond smile. "It's absolutely wonderful."

By the time Ming got Emma settled into Nathan's car and returned to the church, half the guests had made it through the reception line and had spilled onto the street. Since she wasn't the immediate family of the bride and groom, she stood off to one side and waited until the wedding party was free so she could tell them what had happened to Nathan and Emma.

"The contractions seemed fairly close together," Ming said in answer to Susan Case's question regarding Emma's labor. "She said she'd started having them this morning, so I don't know how far along she is."

"Hopefully Nathan will call us from the hospital and let us know," Max's father said.

Sebastian nodded. "I'm sure he will."

"In the meantime," Max said, smiling down at his glowing wife, "we have a reception to get to."

A limo awaited them at the curb to take the group to The Corinthian, a posh venue in downtown Houston's historical district. Ming had never attended an event there, but she'd heard nothing but raves from Missy and Emma. And they were right. The space took its name from the fluted Corinthian columns that flanked the long colonnade where round tables of ten had been placed for the reception. Once the lobby for the First National Bank, the hall's thirty-five-foot ceilings and tall windows now made it an elegant place to hold galas, wedding receptions and lavish birthday parties.

Atop burgundy damask table cloths, gold silverware flanked gilded chargers and white china rimmed with gold. Flickering votive candles in glass holders nestled amongst flowers in Rachel's chosen palette of gold, yellow and deep orange.

Ming had never seen anything so elegant and inviting.

"Susan really outdid herself," Missy commented as she and her husband stopped beside Ming to admire the view. "It almost makes me wish Sebastian and I hadn't run off to Las Vegas to get married." She grinned up at her handsome husband. "Of course, having to wait months to become his wife wouldn't have been worth all this."

Sebastian lifted her hand and brushed a kiss across her knuckles. The heat that passed between them in that moment made Ming blink.

She cleared her throat. "So, you don't regret eloping?"

Missy shook her head, her gaze still locked on her husband's face. "Having a man as deliberate and cautious as Sebastian jump impulsively into a life-changing event as big as marriage was the most amazing, romantic, sexy thing ever."

"He obviously knew what he wanted," Ming murmured, her gaze straying to where Jason laughed with Max's father.

Sebastian's deep voice resonated with conviction as he said, "Indeed I did."

Twelve

Keeping Ming's green-clad form in view as she chatted with their friends, Jason dialed his brother's cell. Evan hadn't mentioned skipping the wedding, and it was out of character for him to just not show. When voice mail picked up, Jason left a message. Then he called his dad, but Tony hadn't heard from Evan, either. Buzzing with concern, Jason slid the phone back into his pocket and headed for Ming.

She was standing alone, her attention on the departing Sebastian and Missy, a wistful expression on her face. Their happiness was tangible. Like a shot to his head, Jason comprehended Ming's fascination. Despite her insistence that she wasn't cut out for marriage, it's what she longed for. Evan had ended their engagement and broken her heart in the process. Her decision to become a single mom was Ming's way of coping with loneliness.

How had he not understood this before? Probably because he didn't want it to be true. He hated to think that she'd find someone new to love and he'd lose her all over again.

Over dinner, while Rachel and Max indulged the guests by kissing at every clinking of glassware, Jason pondered his dinner companion and where the future would take them after tonight. He'd been happier in the past couple of weeks than he'd been in years. It occurred to him just how much he'd missed the closeness that had marked their relationship through high school.

He wasn't ready to give up anything that he'd won. He wanted Ming as the best friend whom he shared his hopes and fears with. He wanted endless steamy nights with the sexy temptress who haunted his dreams. Most of all, he wanted the family that the birth of their baby would create.

All without losing the independence he was accustomed to.

Impossible.

He wasn't foolish enough to think Ming would happily go along with what he wanted, so it was up to Jason to figure out how much he was comfortable giving up and for her to decide what she was willing to live with.

By the time the dancing started, Jason had his proposition formed. Tonight was for romance. Tomorrow morning over breakfast he would tell her his plan and they would start hashing out a strategy.

"Hmm," she murmured as they swayed together on the dance floor. "It's been over a decade since we danced together. I'd forgotten how good you are at this."

"There are things I'm even better at." He executed a spin that left her gasping with laughter. "How soon can we get out of here?"

"It's barely nine." She tried to look shocked, but her eyes glowed at his impatience.

"It's the bride and groom's party." In the crush on the dance floor, he doubted if anyone would notice his hand venturing over her backside. "They have to stick around. We can leave anytime."

Her body quivered, but she grabbed his hand and repositioned it on her waist. "I don't think Max and Rachel would appreciate us ducking out early."

Jason glanced toward the happy newlyweds. "I don't think they'll even notice."

But in the end, they stayed until midnight and saw Max and Rachel off. The newlyweds were spending the night at a downtown hotel and flying on Monday to Gulf Shores, Alabama, where Max owned a house. The location had seemed an odd choice to Jason until he heard the story of how Max and Rachel met in the beach town five years earlier.

As the guests enjoyed one last dance, Jason slid his palm into the small of Ming's back. "Did your sister say anything about Evan's plan to miss the wedding today?"

A line appeared between Ming's finely drawn eyebrows. "No. Did you try calling him?"

"Yes. And I spoke with my dad, too. He hadn't heard from him. This just isn't like Evan."

"Let me call Lily and see if she knows what's going on." Ming dialed her sister's cell and waited for her to pick up. "Evan didn't make the wedding. Did he tell you he was planning on skipping it?" Ming met Jason's eyes and shook her head.

"Find out when she last spoke to him."

"Jason wants to know when you last heard from him. I'm going to put you on speaker, okay?"

"Last night."

It was odd for his brother to go a whole day without talking to one of them. "Is something going on with him?"

"Last night he proposed." Lily sounded miserable.

"Wow," Ming exclaimed, her excitement sounding genuine.

"I told him I couldn't marry him."

Anxiety kicked Jason in the gut. "I guess I don't need to ask how he took that."

Twice he'd seen Evan slip into the same self-destructiveness their father had once exhibited. The first time as a senior in high school when his girlfriend of three years decided to end things a week after graduation. Evan had spent the entire summer in a black funk. The second time was about a year before he and Ming had started dating. His girlfriend of two years had dumped him and married her ex-boyfriend. But Jason suspected neither of those events had upset Evan to the extent that losing Lily would.

"I don't understand," Ming said. "I thought you loved him."

"I do." Lily's voice shook. "I just can't do that to you."

Ming looked to Jason for help. "I don't blame either of you for finding each other."

While the sisters talked, Jason dialed his brother again. When he heard Evan's voice mail message, he hung up. He'd already left three messages tonight. No need to leave another.

"Do you mind if I stop by Evan's before I head home?" Jason quizzed Ming as he escorted her to where she'd left her car. "I'll feel better if I see that he's all right."

"Sure."

"Just let yourself in. I shouldn't be more than fifteen minutes behind you."

But when he got to his brother's house, he discovered why Evan hadn't made it to the wedding and hadn't called him back. His brother was lying unconscious on his living room floor while an infomercial played on the television.

An open bottle of pain pills was tipped over on the coffee table. Empty. In a flash Jason became a fifteen-year-old again, finding his father passed out in the running car, the garage filled with exhaust. With a low cry, Jason dropped to his knees beside his brother. The steady rise and fall of Evan's chest reassured Jason that his brother wasn't dead. Sweat broke out as he grabbed his brother's shoulder and shook.

"Evan. Damn it. Wake up." His throat locked up as he searched for some sign that his brother was near consciousness. Darkness closed over his vision. He was back in the shadow-filled garage, where poisonous fumes had raked his

throat and filled his lungs. His chest tightened with the need
to cough. His brother couldn't die. He had to wake him. With
both hands on Evan's shoulders, Jason shook him hard. "Evan."

A hand shoved him in the chest, breaking through the walls
of panic that had closed in on Jason.

"Geez, Jason." His brother blinked in groggy confusion.
"What the hell?"

Chest tight, Jason sat on the floor and raked his fingers
through his hair. Relief hadn't hit him yet. He couldn't draw
a full breath. Oxygen deprivation made his head spin. He dug
the heels of his palms against his eyes and felt moisture.

Grabbing the pill bottle, he shook it in his brother's face.
"How many of these did you take?"

"Two. That's all I had."

And if there had been more? Would he have taken them?
"Are you sure?"

Evan batted away his brother's hand. "What the hell is
wrong with you?"

"You didn't make the wedding. So I came over to check on
you. Then I saw you on the floor and I thought…" He couldn't
finish the thought.

"I didn't make the wedding because I wasn't in the mood."

"And these?"

"I went for a bicycle ride this morning to clear my head and
took a spill that messed up my back. That's why I'm lying on
the floor. I seized up."

"I left three messages." Jason's hands trembled in the aftermath of the adrenaline rush. "Why didn't you call me back?"

"I turned my phone off. I didn't want to talk to anyone."
Evan rolled to his side and pushed into a sitting position. "What
are you doing here?"

"Lily said she turned down your proposal. I thought maybe
you'd done something stupid."

But Evan wasn't listening. He sucked in a ragged breath.
"She's afraid it'll hurt her sister if we get married." He blinked

three times in rapid succession. "And she wouldn't listen to me when I said Ming wouldn't be as upset as Lily thinks."

Jason couldn't believe what he was hearing. Was this Evan's way of convincing himself he wasn't the bad guy in this scenario? "How do you figure? It's only been six months since your engagement ended."

Evan got to his feet, and Jason glimpsed frustration in his brother's painful movements. "I know you think I messed up, but I did us both a favor."

"How do you figure?" Jason stood as well, his earlier worry lost in a blast of righteous irritation.

"She wasn't as much in love with me as you think she was."

Jason couldn't believe his brother was trying to shift some of the blame for their breakup onto Ming. "You forget who you're talking to. I know Ming. I saw how happy she was with you."

"Yeah, well. Not as happy as she could have been."

"And whose fault was that?" He spun away from Evan and caught his reflection in the large living room windows. He looked hollow. As if the emotion of a moment before had emptied him of all energy.

"I worked hard at the relationship," he said, his voice dull.

"And Ming didn't?"

A long silence followed his question. When Jason turned around, his brother was sitting on the couch, his head in his hands.

"Ming and I were a mistake. I know that now. It's Lily I love." He lifted his head. His eyes were bleak. "I don't know how I'm supposed to live without her."

Jason winced at his brother's phrasing. His cell rang. Ming was calling.

"Is everything okay with Evan?" The concern in her soft voice was a balm to Jason's battered emotions. "It's been almost a half an hour."

He couldn't tell her what he thought was going on while

Evan could overhear. "He threw his back out in a bicycle-riding accident this morning."

"Oh, no. There should be some ice packs in his freezer."

"I'll get him all squared away and be there in a half an hour."

"Take your time. It's been a long couple of days and I'm exhausted. Wake me when you get here."

He ended the call and found himself smiling at the image of Ming asleep in his bed. This past week without her had been hell. Not seeing her. Touching her. He hadn't been able to get her out of his mind.

"Ming told me to put you on ice." Talking to her had lightened his mood. He needed to get his brother settled so he could get home. "Do you want me to bring the ice packs to you here or upstairs?'

"What the hell do I care?"

Evan's sharp retort wasn't like him. Lily's refusal had hit him hard. Fighting anxiety over his brother's dark mood, Jason bullied Evan upstairs and settled him in his bed. Observing his brother's listless state, Jason was afraid to leave him alone.

"Are you going to be okay?"

Evan glared at him. "Why aren't you gone?"

"I thought maybe I should stick around a bit longer."

"Sounds like Ming is waiting for you." Evan deliberately looked away from Jason, making him wonder if Evan suspected what Jason and Ming had been up to.

"She is."

"Then get out of here."

Jason headed for the door. "I'll be back to check on you in the morning."

"Don't bother. I'd rather be alone."

The fifteen-minute drive home offered Jason little time to process what had happened with Evan. What stood out for him was his brother's despair at losing the woman he loved.

He stepped from his garage into the kitchen, and stood in the dark, listening. The silence soothed him, guided him toward the safe place he'd created inside himself. The walled fortress that kept unsettling emotions at bay.

He glanced around the kitchen and smiled as his gaze landed on the chair where he and Ming had made love for the first time. Just one of the great moments that had happened in this room. In almost every room in the house.

He had dozens of incredible memories featuring Ming, and not one of them would be possible if he hadn't opened the doors to his heart and let himself experience raw, no-holds-barred passion.

But desire he could handle. It was the other strong feelings Ming invoked that plagued him. Being with her these past few weeks had made him as happy as he ever remembered. He couldn't stop imagining a life with her.

And this morning he'd been ready to make his dreams reality.

But all that had changed tonight when he'd mistaken what was going on with Evan and relived the terror of the night he'd found his father in the garage. The fear had been real. His pledge to never fall in love—the decision that had stopped making sense these last few weeks—became rational once more.

He couldn't bear to lose Ming. If they tried being a couple and it didn't work out, the damage done to their friendship might never heal. Could he take that risk?

No.

Jason marched up the stairs, confident that he was making the right decision for both of them. He'd expected to find her in his bed, but the soft light spilling from the room next door drew him to the doorway. In what had been his former den, Ming occupied the rocking chair by the window, a stuffed panda clutched against her chest, her gaze on the crib. Encased in serenity, she'd never looked more beautiful.

"Where's all your stuff?" she asked, her voice barely above a whisper.

"It's in the garage."

Gone was the memorabilia of his racing days. In its place stood a crib, changing table and rocker. The walls had been painted a soft yellow. The bedding draped across the crib had pastel jungle animals parading between palm trees and swinging from vines.

She left the chair and walked toward him past the pictures that had graced her childhood bedroom. He'd gotten them from her parents. Her father was sentimental about things like that.

"Who helped you do this?"

"No one." His arms went around her slim form, pulling her against his thudding heart. He rested his chin on her head. "Except for the paint and new carpet. I hired those out."

"You picked all this out by yourself?"

Jason had never shopped for a Christmas or birthday present without her help, and Ming was obviously having a hard time wrapping her head around what he'd accomplished in such a short time.

"Do you like it?" he prompted, surprised by how much he wanted her approval.

"It's perfect."

Nestled in Jason's arms, Ming wouldn't have believed it was possible to fall any deeper in love with him, but at that moment she did. The room had been crafted with loving care by a guy who was as comfortable in a department store as a cat in a kennel of yapping dogs.

He was an amazing man and he would be a terrific father. She was lucky to have such a good friend.

Jason's arms tightened. "I'm glad you like the room. It turned out better than I expected."

"I love you." The courage to say those words had been building in her ever since Jason told her he wanted to go public about his part in her pregnancy. She'd always been truthful with Jason. She'd be a fool and a coward to hide something so important from him.

He tensed.

She gestured at the room. "Seeing this, I thought…" Well, that wasn't true. She'd been reacting emotionally to Jason's decision to be an active father and to his decorating this room to surprise her. "I want to be more than your best friend. I want to be a family with you and our baby."

Fear that he'd react badly didn't halt her confession. As her love for him strengthened with each day that passed, she knew she was going to bare her soul at some point. It might as well be sooner so they could talk it through. "I know that's not what you want to hear," she continued. "But I can't keep pretending I'm okay with just being your best friend."

When his mouth flattened into a grim line, Ming pulled free of his embrace. Without his warmth, she was immediately chilled. She rubbed her arms, but the cold she felt came from deep inside.

"Evan knew how you felt, didn't he?" Jason made it sound like an accusation. "Tonight. He told me you weren't as in love with him as I thought."

"Why did he tell you that?"

"I assumed because he was justifying falling for Lily."

"I swear I never gave him any reason to suspect how I felt about you. I couldn't even admit it to myself until I saw you crash. You've always been so determined not to fall in love or get married." Ming's eyes burned as she spoke. "I knew you'd never let yourself feel anything more for me than friendship, so I bottled everything up and almost married your brother because I was completely convinced you and I could never be."

He was silent a long time. "I haven't told you what happened with Evan tonight."

"Is he okay?"

"When I got to his house I found him on the floor with an empty bottle of painkillers beside him. I thought he was so upset over Lily refusing to marry him that he tried to kill himself."

Ming's heart squeezed in sympathy. The wound he'd suffered when he'd found his father in the garage with the car running had cut deeper than anyone knew. The damage had been permanent. Something Jason would never be free from.

"Did he?" She'd been with Evan for three years and had never seen any sign of depression, but Jason's concern was so keen, she was ready to believe her ex-fiancé had done something to harm himself.

"No. He'd only taken a couple." A muscle jumped in Jason's jaw. He stared at the wall behind her, his gaze on a distant place. "I've never seen him like this. He's devastated that Lily turned him down."

"They're not us."

"What does that mean?" Annoyance edged his voice, warning her that he wasn't in the mood to listen.

She refused to be deterred. "Just because they might not be able to make it work doesn't mean we can't."

"Maybe. But I don't want to take the risk." He gripped her hands and held on tight.

"Have you considered what will happen if we go down that road and it doesn't work out between us? You could come to hate me. I don't want to lose my best friend."

Ming had thought about it, but she had no easy answer. "I don't want to lose you, either, but I'm struggling to think of you as just my best friend. What I feel for you is so much deeper and stronger than that."

And here's where things got tricky. She could love Jason to the best of her ability, but he was convinced that loving someone meant opening up to overwhelming loss, and she couldn't force him to accept something different. But she could make him face what he feared most.

"I love you," she said, her voice brimming with conviction. "I need you to love me in return. I know you do. I feel it every time you touch me." She paused to let her words sink in. "And because we love each other, whether you want to admit it or not, our friendship is altered. We're no longer just best friends. We're a whole lot more."

Through her whole speech he regarded her with an unflinching stare. Now he spoke. "So, what are you saying?"

"I'm saying what you're trying to preserve by not moving our relationship forward no longer exists."

A muscle jumped in his jaw as he stared at her. Silence surrounded them.

"Is this an ultimatum?"

Was it? When she started, she hadn't meant it to be.

"No. It's a statement of intent. Our friendship as it once was is over. I love you and I want us to be a family."

"And if I don't accept that things have to change?"

She made no attempt to hide her sadness. "Then we both lose."

Half an hour after her conversation with Jason, Ming plopped onto her window seat and stared at the dark backyard. She didn't bother changing into a nightgown and sliding between the sheets. What was the point when there was no way she was going to be able to sleep? Her conversation with Jason played over and over in her mind.

Could she have handled it better? Probably not. Jason was never going to relish hearing the truth. He liked their relationship exactly the way it was. Casual. Comfortable. Constant. No doubt he'd resent her for shaking things up.

Dawn found her perched on a stool at the breakfast bar, her gaze on the pool in her backyard. She cradled a cup of coffee in her hands.

"You're up early." Lily entered the kitchen and made a beeline for the cupboard where she kept the ingredients for her healthy breakfast shake. "Couldn't sleep?"

"You're an idiot." Ming knew it wasn't fair to take her frustration out on her sister, but Lily was throwing away love.

Her sister leaned back against the countertop. "Good morning to you, too."

"I'm sorry." Ming shook her head. Her heart hurt. "I'm sitting here thinking how lucky you are that Evan wants to marry you. And it just makes me so mad that you turned him down."

"Are you sure that's what you're mad about?"

Ming blinked and focused her gaze on Lily. "Of course."

"The whole time you were with Evan I was miserable."

Seeing where her sister was going, Ming laughed. "And you think I'm unhappy because Evan loves you?"

"Are you?"

"Not even a little."

"Then why are you so upset?"

With shaky hands, Ming set her cup down and rubbed her face. "I'm pregnant."

After all the arguments she'd had with her sister, the last thing Ming expected was for Lily to rush over and hug her. Ming's throat closed.

"Aren't you going to scold me for doing the wrong thing?" Ming asked.

"I'm sorry I've been so unsupportive. It wasn't fair of me to impose my opinions on you. I'm really happy for you." Lily sounded sincere. "Why didn't you didn't tell me you'd gone to the clinic?"

"Because I didn't go."

"Then how...?" Lily's eyes widened. "Jason?"

"Yes." Ming couldn't believe how much it relieved her to share the truth.

"Have you thought about what this is going to do to Evan?" It was natural that this would be Lily's reaction. She loved Evan and wanted to protect him.

"I was more worried about it before I knew he'd moved on with you." Ming crossed her arms. "But now you've turned down his proposal, and neither Jason nor I want to keep his involvement a secret."

"Why did you have to pick Jason?" Lily shook her head.

Ming refrained from asking Lily why Evan had picked her. "When I decided to have a baby, I wasn't keen on having a stranger's child. Jason understood, and because he's my best friend, he agreed to help."

"So you slept with him."

Ming's cheeks grew warm. "Yes."

"Does that mean you two are a couple?"

"No. As much as I want more, I understood that us being together was a temporary thing. Once I got pregnant, we'd stop."

"But now you're in love with him." Not a question, a statement. "Does he know?"

"I told him last night."

Lily squeezed Ming's hands. "How did he react?"

"Exactly how I'd expected him to." Ming put on her bravest smile. "He has his reasons for never falling in love."

"What are you talking about? He loves you."

"I know, but he won't admit to anything stronger than friendship."

"A friend he wants to sleep with." Lily's smile was wry.

"We have some pretty fabulous chemistry." The chuckle that vibrated in Ming's chest was bittersweet. "But he won't let it become anything more."

"Oh, Ming."

"It's not as if I didn't know how he feels." Ming slid off her stool and looped her arm through Lily's. She tugged her sister toward the stairs. "It just makes it that much more important for you to accept Evan's proposal." Closing her ears to her sister's protests, Ming packed Lily an overnight bag and herded her into the garage. "One of us deserves to be madly in love."

Fifteen minutes later, they pulled up in front of Evan's house. The longing on Lily's face told Ming she'd been right to meddle. She scooped up her sister's overnight bag and breezed up the front walk, Lily trailing slowly behind.

"Are you sure about this?" Lily questioned as they waited for Evan to answer the door.

"Positive. What a horrible sister I would be to stand in the way of your happiness."

Evan opened his door and leaned on it. He looked gray beneath his tan. "Ming? What are you doing here?"

"My sister tells me she turned down your marriage proposal."

His gaze shot beyond Ming to where Lily lingered at the bottom of his steps, but he said nothing.

Not being able to fix what was wrong in her own love life didn't mean she couldn't make sure Lily got her happily-ever-after. "She claims she turned you down because she thinks I would be hurt, but I'm moving on with my life and I don't want to be her excuse for not marrying you." Ming fixed her ex-fiancé with a steely gaze. "Do you promise you'll love her forever?"

"Of course." Evan was indignant.

Fighting to keep her composure intact, Ming headed down the steps to hug her sister. Confident they were out of Evan's hearing, she whispered, "Don't you dare come home until you've got an engagement ring on your finger."

Lily glanced at Evan. "Are you going to take your own advice and go talk to Jason?"

Ming shook her head. "Too much has happened over the last few days. We both need some time to adjust."

"He'll come around. You'll see."

But Ming didn't see. She merely nodded to pacify her sister. "I hope you're right."

Finding Evan passed out last night had reaffirmed to Jason how much better off he was alone. After such a powerful incident, Ming was convinced he'd never change his mind.

"Hey, Dad." It was late Sunday morning when Jason opened his front door and found his father standing there. "What's up?"

"Felt like having lunch with you."

From his father's serious expression, Jason wondered what he was in for, but he grabbed his keys and locked the house. "Where to?"

"Where else?"

They drove to his dad's favorite restaurant, where the pretty brunette hostess greeted Tony by name and flirted with him the whole way to the table.

"She's young enough to be your daughter," Jason commented, eyeing his father over the menu.

Tony chuckled. "She's young enough to be my granddaughter. And there's nothing going on. I love my wife."

When Tony had first announced that he was marrying Claire, Jason had a hard time believing his father had let himself fall in love again. But he'd reasoned that fifteen years of grieving was more than enough for anyone, and there was no question that Claire made his father happy. But his father's optimistic attitude toward love didn't stop Jason from wondering what would happen if Claire left.

Would his father collapse beneath the weight of sadness again? There was no way to know, and Jason hoped he never had to find out. "So, what's on your mind, Dad?"

"I spoke with Evan earlier today. Sounds like he and Lily are engaged."

"Since when?"

"Since this morning. Apparently Ming dropped her sister off and told her not to come home until she was engaged." Tony grinned. "I always loved that girl."

"Good for Evan. He was pretty beat up about Lily last night."

"He said you weren't doing too great, either."

Jason grimaced. "I found Evan on his living room floor, an empty bottle of pain pills next to him and I assumed…"

"That he'd tried to kill himself the way I had when you were fifteen." Tony looked older than his sixty-two years. The vibrancy had gone out of his eyes and the muscles in his face were slack. "That was the single darkest moment of my life, and I'm sorry you had to be the one to experience it with me."

"If I hadn't you'd be dead." They'd never really talked about what had happened. As a teenager Jason had been too shocked by almost losing a second parent to demand answers. And since Evan had been away at college, the secret had remained between Jason and his father while questions ate away Jason's sense of security.

"Looking back, I can't believe I allowed myself to sink so low, but I wasn't aware that I needed help. All I could see was a black pit with steep sides that I couldn't climb out of. Every day the hole seemed deeper. The company was months away from layoffs. I was taking my professional worries out on your mother, and that was eating me up. Then the car accident snatched her and Marie away from us. I was supposed to have driven them to the dress rehearsal for Marie's recital that night, but I was delayed at the office." Tony closed his eyes for a few seconds before resuming. "Those files could have waited until morning. If I had put my family first, they might still be alive. And in the end, all my work came to nothing. The job we'd bid went elsewhere and the company was on the verge of going under. I was to the point where I couldn't live with my failure as a husband, father or businessman."

So, this was the burden his father had carried all these years. Guilt had driven him to try to take his life because he'd perceived himself a failure?

And just like that, Jason's doctrine citing the dangers of falling in love lost all support.

"I thought you were so desperately in love with Mom that you couldn't bear to live without her anymore."

"Her death was devastating, but it wasn't why I started drinking or why I reached the point where I didn't want to go on. It was the guilt." His father regarded Jason in dismay. "Is that why you and Ming never dated? Were you afraid you'd lose her one day?"

"We didn't date because we're friends."

"But you love her."

"Of course I love her." And he did. "She's my—"

His father interrupted to finish. "Best friend." He shook his head in disgust. "Evan had another bit of news for me." Tony leaned his forearms on the table and pinned Jason with hard eyes. "Something Lily told him about Ming."

Now Jason knew why his father had shown up at his house. "She's pregnant."

"And?"

"The baby's mine."

So was Ming. His. Just as he'd told her the night of Max's bachelor party. He'd claimed her and then pushed her away because of a stupid pledge he'd made at fifteen. Had he really expected her to remain his best friend just because that's how it had always been for them?

And now that he knew the truth behind his father's depression, Jason could admit that he wanted the same things she did. Marriage. Children. The love of a lifetime.

But after he pushed her away last night, would she still want those things with him?

Jason's chair scraped the floor as he got to his feet. He threw enough money on the table to cover their tab and gestured for his father to get up. "We have to go."

"Go where?" Tony followed his son out the door without receiving an answer. "Go where?" he repeated, sliding behind the wheel of his BMW.

"I have an errand to run. Then I'm going to go see Ming. It's way past time I tell her how I really feel."

Ming swam beneath the pool's surface, stroking hard to reach the side before her breath gave out. After leaving Evan's house hours earlier, she'd been keyed up. After cleaning her refrigerator and vacuuming the whole upstairs, she'd decided to burn off her excess energy, hoping the cool water would calm both her body and her mind.

The exercise did its job. By the time she'd completed her twentieth lap, her thoughts had stopped racing. Muffin awaited her at the edge of the pool. As soon as Ming surfaced, the Yorkie raced forward and touched her nose to Ming's. The show of affection made her smile.

"What would I do without you?" she asked the small dog and received a lick in response.

"I've been asking myself the same question since you left last night."

A shadow fell across her. Ming looked up, her stomach flipping at the determined glint in Jason's blue eyes. Relief raced through her. The way their conversation had ended the previous night, she'd worried their friendship was irrevocably damaged.

"Luckily you aren't ever going to find that out." She accepted Jason's hand and let him pull her out of the water.

He wrapped her in a towel and pulled her against him. Dropping his lips to hers, he kissed her slow and deep. Ming tossed aside all the heartache of the past twelve hours and surrendered to the powerful emotions Jason aroused.

"I was wrong to dump all that stuff about Evan on you last night," he told her.

"I'm your friend. You know I'm always there for you."

"I know I take that for granted."

He took her by the hand and led her inside. To Ming's delight he pulled her toward the stairs. This wasn't what she'd expected from him after she confessed her feelings. She figured he'd distance himself from her as he'd done with women in the past.

But when they arrived in her bedroom, he didn't take her in his arms or rip the covers off the mattress and sweep her onto the soft sheets.

Instead, he kissed her on the forehead. "Grab a shower. I have an errand to run and could use your help."

An errand? Disappointment sat like a bowling ball in her stomach. "What sort of an errand?"

"I never got Max and Rachel a wedding present."

"Oh, Jason." She rolled her eyes at him.

"I'm hopeless without you," he reminded her, nudging her in the direction of the bathroom. "You know that."

"Does it have to be today?"

"They're leaving for Alabama tomorrow morning. I want them to have it before then." He scooped up the Yorkshire terrier and the dog's stuffed squirrel toy. "Muffin and I will be waiting for you downstairs."

"Fine."

Half an hour later Ming descended her stairs and found Jason entertaining Muffin with a game of fetch. She'd put on a red sundress with thin straps and loved the way Jason's eyes lit up in appreciation.

She collected the Yorkie's leash and her purse and headed out the front door. When she spotted the car in front of her house, she hesitated. "Why are you driving the 'Cuda?"

"I told you, I never got Max and Rachel a wedding present."

Understanding dawned. "You're giving him back the car?"

"The bet we made seems pretty stupid in light of recent events."

"What recent events?"

He offered her his most enigmatic smile. "Follow me and you'll find out."

When they arrived at Max and Rachel's house, Jason didn't even have a chance to get out of the car before the front door opened. To his amusement, Max looked annoyed.

"Why are you driving the 'Cuda?" he demanded as Jason slowly got to his feet. "Do you have any idea what the car's worth?"

"I don't, since you never told me what you paid for it." Jason took Ming's hand as she reached his side and pulled her close.

"Look, I'm sorry that I didn't get you anything for your wedding. Ming was supposed to help me pick something, but she backed out at the last minute."

"Jason." She bumped her hip against him in warning. "You are perfectly capable of shopping on your own."

"No, he's not," Max put in.

"No, I'm not. So, here." Jason held out the keys.

"You're giving me back the 'Cuda?" Max's thunderstruck expression was priceless.

"I realize now that I had an unfair advantage when we made the bet. You were already in love with Rachel, just too stubborn to realize it."

Max took the keys and nodded. "Being stubborn when it comes to love means you lose out on all sorts of things."

Jason felt the barb hit home. He had missed a lot with Ming. If he hadn't been so determined never to be hurt, she might have married his brother, and Jason could have ended up with a lifetime of pain.

Rachel had come out to join them. She snuggled against her husband's side and looked fondly at the bright yellow car. "What's going on?"

"Jason's giving me back the 'Cuda," Max explained with a wry grin. "Can I interest you in a ride?"

To Jason's surprise, the blonde's cheeks turned pink. Unwilling to delve too deeply into whatever subtext had just passed between husband and wife, he reached for the passenger seat and pulled out a box wrapped in white-and-silver paper and adorned with a silver bow.

"And because the car is a really lousy wedding present," he continued, handing the gift to Rachel, "I got this for you."

Rachel grinned. "I think the car is a lovely present, but thank you for this."

Jason shut the 'Cuda's door and gave the car one last pat. "Take good care of her," he told Max.

"I intend to." Max leaned down and planted a firm kiss on his wife's lips.

"I meant the car," Jason retorted, amused.

"Her, too."

After spending another ten minutes with the newlyweds, Ming and Jason returned to her car.

"What was that about?" she asked, standing beside the driver's door. "You didn't need me to help deliver the car. You could have had Max come pick it up."

"It was symbolic." He could feel her tension growing and decided he'd better tell her what was on his mind before she worked herself into a lather. "I won the car because I bet against love. It sits in my garage, a testament to my stubbornness and stupidity. So I decided to give it back to Max. Apparently in addition to its financial value it has some sentimental value to him, as well."

Her lips curved. "I'm happy to hear you admit that you were idiotic and pigheaded, but what caused your enlightenment?"

He leaned against the car and drew her into his arms.

"My dad swung by my house earlier and we had a long talk about what happened after my mother and sister died."

She sighed and relaxed against him. "You've talked with him about it before, haven't you?"

"We talked about his depression, but I never understood what was at the root of him trying to take his life."

"I thought it was because he was so much in love with your mom that he couldn't live without her."

"That's what I believed. Turns out I didn't know the whole story."

"There's more?"

"Today I found out why he was so depressed after my mother and sister died. Apparently he stayed at work when he was supposed to drive them the night they died. He thinks if he'd chosen his family over the business they might still be alive. It was eating him up."

"You mean he felt guilty?"

Jason nodded. "Guilty because he'd failed her. Not devastated by loss. All these years I was wrong to think love only led to pain." He watched Ming's expression to gauge her reaction to his tale. "When my dad fell in love with Claire, I thought he was nothing more than an optimistic fool." Jason winced. He'd spoken up against his father marrying her and a rift had formed between them. "Then Max fell in love with Rachel. Until he met her, he'd had a block of ice where his heart should be."

"But Rachel's great."

Jason nodded. "And she's perfect for Max, but when he fell head over heels for her, I was even more convinced that love made everyone else crazy and that I was the only sane one."

It scared her how firmly he clung to his convictions. "And now your brother has gone mad for Lily."

"That he has." He gave her a sheepish smile. "Max and his brothers. My dad. Evan. They're all so damned happy."

"You're happy."

"When I'm with you." He set his forehead against hers. "I've been a stubborn idiot. All this time I've been lying to myself about what I wanted. I thought if you and I made love, I could keep things the way they were between us and manage to have the best of both worlds."

"Only I had to go and fall in love with you."

"No. You had to go and tell me you wanted us to be together as a family." At last he was free to share with her what lay in his heart. "Did you know when you chose me to help you get pregnant that a baby would bind us together forever?"

"It crossed my mind, but that isn't why I decided on you." She frowned defensively. "And I'd like to point out that you agreed to help me. You also had to realize that any child I gave birth to would be part of us."

"From the instant you said you wanted me to be your baby's father, all I could think about was how much I wanted you." He took her hand and kissed her palm, felt her tension ease.

"After prom night I ran from the way I felt about you. It went against everything I believed. I've been running for the last fifteen years."

"And what is it you want?"

"You. More than anything. Marry me. I want to spend the rest of my life showing you how much I love you." He produced a diamond ring and held it before her eyes.

Heart pounding, she stared at the fiery gem as he took her left hand and slid the ring onto her finger. It fit perfectly.

"Yes. Yes. Of course, yes."

Before she finished her fervent acceptance, he kissed her. As his lips moved with passionate demand against hers, she melted beneath the rush of desire. He took his time demonstrating how much he loved her until his breath was rough and ragged. At last he lifted his head and stared into her eyes. Her stark joy stopped his heart.

Grinning, he hugged her hard. "And just in case you're worried about everyone's reaction, I cleared this with your sister and parents and my brother. The consensus seems to be that it's about time we take things from friends…"

"To forever." She laughed, a glorious sound of joy. "How lucky can a girl be?" she murmured. "I get to marry my best friend and the man I adore."

Jason cupped her face and kissed her gently. "What could be better than that?"

Ming lifted onto her tiptoes and wrapped her arms around his neck. "Not one single thing."

Epilogue

One year later

Bright afternoon sunshine glinted off the brand new paint on the galaxy blue Mustang parked in the driveway. Ming adjusted the big red bow attached to the roof and waved goodbye to the Stover brothers, who'd dropped the repaired race car off moments before. With her anniversary present for Jason looking absolutely perfect, she glanced toward the colonial's front door. The delivery had not been particularly quiet and she was surprised her husband of one year hadn't come out to see what the commotion was about.

She headed inside and paused in the foyer. From the family room came the sounds of revving engines so she followed the sound. Jason sat on the couch in front of the sixty-inch TV, absorbed in a NASCAR race. Muffin slept on the back of the couch near his shoulder.

"Jason?"

Muffin's head came up and her tail wagged, but Jason didn't

react at all. She circled the couch and discovered why he hadn't heard the delivery. He was fast asleep. So were their twin three-month-old sons, Jake and Connor, one on either side of him, snuggled into the crooks of his arms.

Ming grinned at the picture of her snoozing men and hoped this nap meant Jason would have lots of energy later tonight because she had plans for him that required his full strength. But right now she was impatient to show him his gift.

"Jason." She knelt between his knees and set her hands on his thighs. Muffin stretched and jumped down to lick Connor's cheek. "Wake up and see what I got you for our anniversary." When her words didn't rouse him, she slid her palms up his thigh. She was more than halfway toward her goal when his lips twitched upward at the corners.

"Keep going."

"Later."

He sighed, but didn't open his eyes. "That's what you always say." But despite his complaint, his smile had blossomed into a full-blown grin.

"And I always come through." She stood and slapped his knee. "Now come see your present."

She scooped up Jake and waited until Jason draped Connor over his shoulder and got to his feet before she headed back through the house. Muffin raced ahead of them to the foyer. Tingling with anticipation, Ming pulled open the front door and stepped aside so Jason could look out. The shock on his face when he spotted the car was priceless.

"You had the Mustang repaired?" He wrapped his free arm around her waist and pulled her tight against him.

"I did." She smiled up at him and his lips dropped onto hers for a passion-drenched kiss that curled her toes. When he let her breath again, she caught his hand and dragged him down the steps. "I think you should start racing again."

He hadn't been anywhere near the track since he'd crashed the Mustang over a year ago. Between getting married, her taking over the dental practice and the birth of their twins, they'd been plenty busy.

"Are you sure that's what you want?" Jason ran his hand along the front fender with the same appreciation he'd lavished on her thigh the previous night. "It'll take me away some weekends."

"I never wanted you to stop doing what you love."

"What I love is being your husband and a father to Jake and Connor."

"And I love that, too." She nudged her body against his. "But racing is your passion, and Max is bored to death without you to compete against."

He coasted his palm over her hip and cupped her butt, drawing her up on her toes for a slow, thorough kiss. The babies began to fuss long before Ming was done savoring her husband's fabulous technique and they broke apart with matching regretful sighs.

"More of that to come later," she assured him, soothing Jake.

While they were distracted, a car had pulled up behind the Mustang. Max and Rachel got out. "Get a room you two," Max called good-naturedly, picking up the excited terrier.

"That's the plan," Ming retorted, handing off her son to Rachel.

"Great to see you guys." Jason switched Connor to his other arm so he could give Max a man hug. "Are you staying for dinner?"

"They're staying," Ming said. "We're leaving. They're going to babysit while we celebrate our anniversary." Since the twins were born, uninterrupted time together was pretty much non-existent, and Ming was determined that she and Jason should make a memorable start to their second year of marriage.

Jason eyed Max. "Are you sure you're up for this?"

"I think I could use a little parenting practice."

"I'm pregnant," Rachel announced, beaming.

While Jason congratulated Max, and Rachel cooed over

Jake, Ming marveled at her good fortune. She'd married her best friend and they had two healthy baby boys. Her practice was thriving. Lily and Evan were getting married in the spring. Everything that had been going wrong a little over a year ago was now sorted out. It wasn't perfect, but it was wonderful.

Jason looked over and caught her watching him. The blaze that kindled in his eyes lit an answering inferno deep inside her. For twenty-five years he'd been her best friend and that had been wonderful, but for the rest of her life he was going to be her husband and that was perfect.

* * * * *

COMING NEXT MONTH from Harlequin Desire®
AVAILABLE MARCH 5, 2013

#2215 BEGUILING THE BOSS
Rich, Rugged Ranchers
Joan Hohl
Rancher Marshall Grainger doesn't trust women...even though he's not averse to bedding them. Will a paper marriage with his live-in assistant make him change his ways?

#2216 A WEDDING SHE'LL NEVER FORGET
Daughters of Power: The Capital
Robyn Grady
When a socialite wedding planner gets amnesia, she forgets all about her previous staid, formal ways and falls for the Aussie billionaire who's her complete opposite!

#2217 ONE SECRET NIGHT
The Master Vintners
Yvonne Lindsay
Can a man who is master of all love a woman who cannot be mastered? And can he trust her to keep a family secret after their night of passion?

#2218 THE THINGS SHE SAYS
Kat Cantrell
He's her knight in shining armor driving a *muy amarillo* Ferrari. She's a small-town waitress running away. Will their passion-filled Texas road trip lead to heartbreak or happily ever after?

#2219 BEHIND PALACE DOORS
Jules Bennett
Friendship quickly turns to passion when a Greek prince and his best friend enter a marriage of convenience. But can the known playboy ever fall in love for real?

#2220 A TRAP SO TENDER
The Drummond Vow
Jennifer Lewis
James and Fiona are used to getting what they want. Each secretly plans to use the other to obtain their goal—until they make the mistake of losing their hearts.

You can find more information on upcoming Harlequin®
titles, free excerpts and more at www.Harlequin.com.

HDCNM0213

REQUEST YOUR FREE BOOKS!
2 FREE NOVELS PLUS 2 FREE GIFTS!

HARLEQUIN®

Desire

ALWAYS POWERFUL, PASSIONATE AND PROVOCATIVE

YES! Please send me 2 FREE Harlequin Desire® novels and my 2 FREE gifts (gifts are worth about \$10). After receiving them, if I don't wish to receive any more books, I can return the shipping statement marked "cancel." If I don't cancel, I will receive 6 brand-new novels every month and be billed just \$4.30 per book in the U.S. or \$4.99 per book in Canada. That's a savings of at least 14% off the cover price! It's quite a bargain! Shipping and handling is just 50¢ per book in the U.S. and 75¢ per book in Canada.* I understand that accepting the 2 free books and gifts places me under no obligation to buy anything. I can always return a shipment and cancel at any time. Even if I never buy another book, the two free books and gifts are mine to keep forever.

225/326 HDN FVP7

Name	(PLEASE PRINT)	
Address		Apt. #
City	State/Prov.	Zip/Postal Code

Signature (if under 18, a parent or guardian must sign)

Mail to the **Harlequin® Reader Service:**
IN U.S.A.: P.O. Box 1867, Buffalo, NY 14240-1867
IN CANADA: P.O. Box 609, Fort Erie, Ontario L2A 5X3

Want to try two free books from another line?
Call 1-800-873-8635 or visit www.ReaderService.com.

* Terms and prices subject to change without notice. Prices do not include applicable taxes. Sales tax applicable in N.Y. Canadian residents will be charged applicable taxes. Offer not valid in Quebec. This offer is limited to one order per household. Not valid for current subscribers to Harlequin Desire books. All orders subject to credit approval. Credit or debit balances in a customer's account(s) may be offset by any other outstanding balance owed by or to the customer. Please allow 4 to 6 weeks for delivery. Offer available while quantities last.

Your Privacy—The Harlequin® Reader Service is committed to protecting your privacy. Our Privacy Policy is available online at www.ReaderService.com or upon request from the Harlequin Reader Service.

We make a portion of our mailing list available to reputable third parties that offer products we believe may interest you. If you prefer that we not exchange your name with third parties, or if you wish to clarify or modify your communication preferences, please visit us at www.ReaderService.com/consumerschoice or write to us at Harlequin Reader Service Preference Service, P.O. Box 9062, Buffalo, NY 14269. Include your complete name and address.

HDI3

SPECIAL EXCERPT FROM
HARLEQUIN® DESIRE™

Can one wrong turn lead to happily ever after?

2012 So You Think You Can Write winner

Kat Cantrell

presents

THE THINGS SHE SAYS

Available March 2013 from Harlequin Desire!

The only thing worse than being lost was being lost in Texas. In August.

Kris Demetrious slumped against the back of his screaming yellow Ferrari and peeled the shirt from his damp chest.

What had possessed him to drive to Dallas instead of fly?

A stall tactic, that's what.

He sighed as bright afternoon sun beat down, a thousand times hotter than it might have been if he'd been wearing a color other than black.

Just then, a dull orange pickup truck, coated with rust, drove through the center of a dirt cloud and braked on the shoulder behind the Ferrari. After a beat, the truck's door creaked open and light hit the faded logo: Big Bobby's Garage. Cracked boots appeared and *whoomped* to the ground. Out of the settling dust, a small figure emerged.

"Car problems, Chief?" she drawled as she approached.

Her Texas accent was as thick as the dust, but her voice rolled out musically. She slipped off her sunglasses, and the world skipped a beat.

The unforgiving heat, lack of road signs and the problems waiting for him in Dallas slid away.

Clear blue eyes peered up at him out of a heart-shaped face and a riot of cinnamon-colored hair curled against porcelain cheeks. She was fresh, innocent and breathtakingly beautiful. Like a living sunflower.

She eyed him. "*¿Problema con el coche, señor?*"

Kris cleared his throat. "I'm Greek, not Hispanic."

"Wow. Yes, you are, with a sexy accent and everything. Say something else," she commanded. The blue of her eyes turned sultry. "Tell me your life is meaningless without me, and you'd give a thousand fortunes to make me yours."

"Seriously?"

She laughed, a pure sound that trilled through his abdomen. A potent addition to the come-hither she radiated like perfume.

"Only if you mean it," she said. With a grin, she jerked her chin. "I'll cut you a break. You can talk about whatever you want. We don't see many fancy foreigners in these parts, but I'd be happy to check out the car. Might be an easy fix."

"It's not broken down. I'm just lost," he clarified.

"Lost, huh?" Her gaze raked over him from top to toe. "Lucky for me I found you, then."

Will Kris make it to Dallas?
Find out in
THE THINGS SHE SAYS

Available March 2013 from Harlequin Desire!

Copyright © 2013 by Katrina Williams

HARLEQUIN

Desire

ALWAYS POWERFUL, PASSIONATE AND PROVOCATIVE.

Rancher Marshall Grainger doesn't trust
women...even though he's not averse to
bedding them. Will a paper marriage with his
live-in assistant make him change his ways?

Look for

BEGUILING THE BOSS

by Joan Hohl.

Rich, Rugged Ranchers:
No woman can resist them!

Available In March wherever books are sold.

**Look for upcoming titles in the
Rich, Rugged Ranchers miniseries.
Available January–June 2013**

HD73228